*Harlequin is 60 years old,
and Harlequin Blaze is celebrating!*

*After all, a lot can happen in 60 years,
or 60 minutes…or 60 seconds!*

*And a lot happens in Blaze's
heart-stopping new miniseries:*

From 0 to 60!

Don't miss:

*A LONG, HARD RIDE
by Alison Kent
March 2009*

*OUT OF CONTROL
by Julie Miller
April 2009*

*HOT-WIRED
by Jennifer LaBrecque
May 2009*

*Going from "Hello" to "How was it?"
doesn't have to take lo*

Dear Reader,

Who can resist celebrating an anniversary? And when it's a big one, it's even better. That's why I was so thrilled to be included in the FROM 0–60 miniseries, Blaze's salute to Harlequin's 60th anniversary.

I was a reader long before I was a writer and I've always appreciated that Harlequin books consistently delivered a fine romance and a guaranteed happy ending. There are times when I still pinch myself, not believing that I'm part of that now. I'm especially happy to be writing for Harlequin Blaze, where women celebrate and embrace their sensuality.

Hot-Wired is particularly special to me, because not only does it celebrate Harlequin's 60th anniversary, it also includes fast cars and the guys who drive them (a weakness of mine). Maybe that's why it was so much fun to write. I hope you have just as much fun reading it!

I love to hear from readers. Be sure to visit my Web site at www.jenniferlabrecque.com and my daily blog at www.soapboxqueens.com.

Enjoy,

Jennifer LaBrecque

Hot-Wired

JENNIFER LaBRECQUE

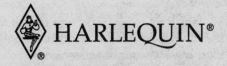

HARLEQUIN®

TORONTO • NEW YORK • LONDON
AMSTERDAM • PARIS • SYDNEY • HAMBURG
STOCKHOLM • ATHENS • TOKYO • MILAN • MADRID
PRAGUE • WARSAW • BUDAPEST • AUCKLAND

If you purchased this book without a cover you should be aware that this book is stolen property. It was reported as "unsold and destroyed" to the publisher, and neither the author nor the publisher has received any payment for this "stripped book."

Recycling programs
for this product may
not exist in your area.

ISBN-13: 978-0-373-79469-0
ISBN-10:   0-373-79469-X

HOT-WIRED

Copyright © 2009 by Jennifer LaBrecque.

All rights reserved. Except for use in any review, the reproduction or utilization of this work in whole or in part in any form by any electronic, mechanical or other means, now known or hereafter invented, including xerography, photocopying and recording, or in any information storage or retrieval system, is forbidden without the written permission of the publisher, Harlequin Enterprises Limited, 225 Duncan Mill Road, Don Mills, Ontario M3B 3K9, Canada.

This is a work of fiction. Names, characters, places and incidents are either the product of the author's imagination or are used fictitiously, and any resemblance to actual persons, living or dead, business establishments, events or locales is entirely coincidental.

This edition published by arrangement with Harlequin Books S.A.

® and TM are trademarks of the publisher. Trademarks indicated with ® are registered in the United States Patent and Trademark Office, the Canadian Trade Marks Office and in other countries.

www.eHarlequin.com

Printed in U.S.A.

ABOUT THE AUTHOR

After a varied career path that included barbecue-joint waitress, corporate numbers cruncher and bug-business maven, Jennifer LaBrecque has found her true calling writing contemporary romance. Named 2001 Notable New Author of the Year and 2002 winner of the prestigious Maggie Award for Excellence, she is also a two-time RITA® Award finalist. Jennifer lives in suburban Atlanta with one husband, one active daughter, one really bad cat, two precocious greyhounds and a Chihuahua who runs the whole show.

Books by Jennifer LaBrecque

HARLEQUIN BLAZE

206—DARING IN THE DARK
228—ANTICIPATION
262—HIGHLAND FLING
367—THE BIG HEAT
401—NOBODY DOES
      IT BETTER
436—YULE BE MINE

HARLEQUIN TEMPTATION

886—BARELY MISTAKEN
904—BARELY DECENT
952—BARELY BEHAVING
992—BETTER THAN
      CHOCOLATE
1012—REALLY HOT!

Don't miss any of our special offers. Write to us at the following address for information on our newest releases.

Harlequin Reader Service
U.S.: 3010 Walden Ave., P.O. Box 1325, Buffalo, NY 14269
Canadian: P.O. Box 609, Fort Erie, Ont. L2A 5X3

Thanks to Brenda Chin and Margaret Learn
for helping me make this a better book.

And to Alison Kent, Julie Miller and Lori Borrill,
all top-notch writers. It was great fun creating
the world of Dahlia, Tennessee. Wish we could
go for a visit.

And last but not least, to all the drag racers and
their crews who devote endless hours to putting
on a great show, especially the ORSCA folks.

1

BEAU STILLWELL could kiss her ass. If she could ever find him, that was.

Her temper beginning to fray at the edges, Natalie Bridges silently huffed and carefully picked her way through yet another row of big pickup trucks, trailers, motor homes and some of the loudest, gaudiest souped-up cars she'd ever had the misfortune to see. Welcome to Dahlia Speedway, where big boys and their toys hurtled down a quarter-mile track to see who could go the fastest. Quite frankly, she didn't get it.

What, or rather who, she needed to get, however, was Beauregard Stillwell. She'd called and left messages every day for two weeks with the secretary of Stillwell Construction. He'd summarily ignored them. She'd doggedly left messages on his cell and home phone. No call back.

She jumped as a car cranked next to her with a near deafening roar. Was there another wedding planner in Nashville, Tennessee, who'd go to these lengths to get the job done? Maybe, maybe not, but she was bound and determined that Caitlyn Stillwell and Cash Vickers would have the wedding of their dreams—if she could ever get Caitlyn's brother, Beau, to cooperate.

Caitlyn and Cash had the *most* romantic story. Call it fate or destiny or karma, but fresh out of college with a degree in film and video, Caitlyn had lucked into shooting a music video for rising country music star Cash Vickers at an antebellum plantation outside Nashville. In a nutshell, they'd fallen in love with each other and the place during the filming. In a wildly romantic gesture, Cash had bought the plantation, Belle Terre, for him and Caitlyn. They both had their hearts set on getting married there. However, while a faintly neglected air worked for a video for "Homesick," a song about finding where you belong and who you belonged there with, it didn't work for a wedding. Caitlyn didn't trust anyone with the renovations except her big brother, Beau.

Which was all good and fine, if Natalie could just get him to talk to her about the renovation schedule. In the two-week span of being ignored, Natalie could've lined up another builder to handle the remodel, except this was a sticking point with Caitlyn. No Beau Stillwell, no remodel. No remodel, no wedding.

And come hell or high water, in which hell might very well take the form of Beau Stillwell, Natalie was planning and executing this wedding. Cash was being touted as country music's next big thing, and being in charge of his and Caitlyn's wedding would set Natalie apart as Nashville's premier wedding planner…but only if everything went off without a hitch. She'd either be ruined or all the rage. Ruined wasn't a viable option.

Hence, she'd finished up the rehearsal dinner for tomorrow's wedding between Gina Morris and Tommy Pitchford, settled them and their families at the private banquet room at the upscale Giancarlo's Ristorante, and left her assistant, Cynthia, to deal with any residual problems. Natalie had driven the thirty miles out of Nashville and parted with twenty dollars at the gate to gain entry to the one place she knew for sure she could find Mr. Stillwell on a Friday evening—the Dahlia drag strip.

Dodging a low-slung orange car with skulls air-brushed on the front and side as it pulled down the "street" in the congested pit area, she thought better a drag strip than a strip joint. Although she had thought it was pretty interesting the one time she'd tracked down a recalcitrant groom and dragged him out of a strip club. Her seldom-seen, inner wild girl had thought she wouldn't mind doing a pole dance for someone special in a private setting.

Even though she was about five unreturned phone calls beyond annoyed, she had to admit the drag strip was an interesting place. Apparently drag racing pit areas were wherever the car's trailer was parked. She tried to ignore the stares and titters that followed her. Maybe three-inch heels and a suit weren't the dress code at the drag strip, but changing would have meant driving all the way back across Nashville when she'd had the girl genius idea of coming here to track down Beau the Bastard, as she and Cynthia had dubbed him earlier today when he'd blown off her call yet again.

She clutched her purse tighter against her side. There was almost a carnival atmosphere. An announcer "called" the race, giving statistics and tidbits about each driver over a loudspeaker. The cars themselves were beyond loud, spectators whooped and hollered, people zoomed around on four-wheelers and golf carts, and there was plenty of tailgating going on at the race trailers. It sort of reminded her of holidays at her parents' house—chaos. Although, unlike at her folks', there was at least some structure and method behind the madness here.

She passed a concession stand located behind the packed spectator bleachers and the smell of hamburgers and French fries wafting out set her mouth watering and her stomach growling, reminding her she hadn't eaten since breakfast. God, she'd kill for a greasy fry dredged in catsup right now—the ultimate comfort food. However, she was probably packing on another five pounds just from smelling them.

She walked away from the people lined up at the burger window. Directly across from the food concession, she noticed a T-shirt vendor displayed his, or her, wares. Natalie nearly laughed aloud at the one that proclaimed "Real Men Do It With 10.5 Inches."

She didn't get the inside joke and it was rude and crude, but still kind of funny. And she had to smile at the "Damn Right It's Fast, Stupid Ass" next to it.

She was so busy laughing at the T-shirts that catching her heel in a crack caught her totally unawares. Arms flailing, she pitched into a guy…carrying a hot dog and a plastic cup of beer.

"Damn, lady," he yelled, "watch where you're going." He shot her a nasty look. "And that cost me my last eight bucks."

Natalie righted herself, dug into her purse, pulled out a ten and shoved it in the man's hand. "Sorry."

Mollified by his two-dollar gain, he changed his tune. "No problem." He looked down her chest and grimaced. "Napkins are over there." He turned on his heel and returned to the concession counter.

She glanced down. Her favorite cream silk blouse with the lovely ruffle down the center clung to her in a beer bath. Bright yellow mustard and red catsup obscured the flowers on the left breast of her jacket. She wasn't sure that blouse and jacket weren't both ruined. She quelled the urge to laugh hysterically. Napkins. She needed napkins.

She started toward the round, bar-height table that held the napkins, along with the hamburger and hot dog fixings, and realized she'd wrenched the heel off her right pump when she'd stepped in the asphalt crack. She limped over to the table and grabbed a napkin.

A blonde with dark roots in jeans and a halter top

gave her a sympathetic look. "The bathroom's right around the corner."

"Thanks."

Five minutes later, she'd managed to work some of the mustard and catsup stain out of her jacket and she'd blotted at her beer-soaked blouse. She'd toyed with, and promptly dismissed, the notion that she'd be better off trading them for one of the graphic tees. No, that would make her look even more bedraggled than her stained clothing.

For the thousandth time, she silently cursed Beau Stillwell. This was all his fault. Maybe he wasn't personally responsible for the asphalt crack she'd caught her heel in, but if he'd had the common courtesy to return just one of her phone calls or, at the very least, left a message for her with his secretary, Natalie wouldn't have been reduced to chasing him all over Dahlia, Tennessee, and her heel wouldn't have gotten stuck in the damn crack in the damn first place because she wouldn't have been here.

She smiled grimly at herself in the chipped mirror and tucked her hair back into what was left of her chignon as best she could. She reapplied a coat of pale pink lipstick and rubbed her lips together. She didn't care what they said on the Style Network— doing that funky top-lip-against-the-bottom-one smear smoothed out the color. Dropping the lipstick tube back in her purse, she stood up straight, squared her shoulders, and gave herself a pep talk.

Granted she fell a little short of the mark—she always aimed to project an elegant professionalism—but she didn't *really* resemble the walking wounded, she reassured herself. And killing Beau Stillwell when she found him, or at least braining him with what was left of her right pump, was not in her best interest. Dead, or even slightly brained, would preclude her nailing him down as to the remodel schedule on Belle Terre, which was why she was standing in the shabby, smelly bathroom of the Dahlia drag strip reeking of beer, mustard and catsup rather than attending Nashville's latest art gallery opening, where she was sure Shadwell Jackson III, the guy who had Prince Charming written all over him, was supposed to be.

Heck yeah, she believed in Prince Charmings and wanted one for herself. How could she be a wedding planner and not believe in happy-ever-after? She was detail-oriented and a devotee of true love—it was a career tailor-made for her.

She came from a long line of happy-ever-afters. She figured it was a genetic thing. No one in either her mother's or her father's families had ever gotten a divorce. And none of them were living in misery. Sure they had problems to work through, but all of them had sound marriages. Her parents were still absolutely in love after thirty-two years, raising Natalie and taking in foster kids on a regular basis.

She'd known for years what her Prince Charming

would be like when he swept her off her feet. She'd always envisioned her Mr. Right as an urbane professional who donned a suit and tie every morning, refined, gallant. And instead of meeting Shad, an imminent candidate for that position, she was here, tracking down pain-in-her-ass Beau Stillwell.

She sucked in a deep, calming breath, which proved a mistake in a public toilet. Blech. She limped back outside where the scent of fast food underpinned the acrid smell of burning rubber. Beau Stillwell, did not know the measure of the woman he was dealing with. She could handle this. She *would* handle this.

Smoothing her hand over her skirt and tweaking her stained jacket into place over her stained blouse, she fixed her best smile on her face rather than a scowl and gimped forward on her broken heel toward the pit area for Stillwell Motors Racing.

She'd employ charm and tact and whip the elusive brother of the bride right into shape.

THE FOUR-WHEELER towed Beau and his '69 Camaro into their pit area beneath the two green pop-up tents next to the trailer. Before he'd even climbed out of the car, his motor guy Darnell and general crew member Tim were pulling the hood pins, eager to read the spark plugs and tweak the setup.

Beau tugged off his helmet and stripped off his neck brace and fireproof gloves. A grin split Scooter Lewis's face as he walked over, waving Beau's run results in his hand. "That was a helluva run. Even with your tires spinning a little off the line, you beat him off the tree and at the sixty-foot. He didn't have a prayer of catching you."

"It was sweet, wasn't it?" Beau said, the adrenalin rush that came with rocketing down a quarter-mile track in less than four and a half seconds was beginning to subside. It was like a five-second orgasm with an unpredictable woman. From the instant the light went green, signaling him to go, he was never sure what would happen on the run, but it was guaranteed to be a rush. "If we run that again tomorrow, we should qualify first."

"I'll ramp it down some and that'll take care of the spin," Darnell said, glancing up and handing off the socket wrench to Tim.

Beau nodded. As crew chief, Scooter oversaw all the adjustments based on track and weather conditions, but Darnell was damn near a genius when it came to motor setups. "Who've we got to beat tomorrow? Mitchell or Taylor?"

"Mitchell. They dropped in a new motor but you're still the better driver."

And without arrogance, Beau knew it was true. Driving a race car was in his blood. He'd been born with a need for speed. It's what the Stillwell men did. His father had raced, his grandfather had raced, and stories of his great-grandfather Theodore Stillwell outrunning prohibitionists in a Model T in his day was local legend around Dahlia, Tennessee. Before that, the Stillwell men were hell at the helm of a buggy. In fact, family rumor had it that Stillwells drove a mean chariot in the day. That, however, was totally unsubstantiated Stillwell family lore.

A couple of fans stopped by to check out the car. Beau recognized the guys as motorheads who showed up at every race. They were still looking over the engine and bending Darnell's ear when a blonde and a brunette in matching jeans and what he'd guess to be double D's in tube tops strolled into the pit area.

"Hi, I'm Sherree," the blonde said, "and this is Tara. Would you take a picture with us?"

"Certainly, ladies." He offered them his most charming smile.

Sherree shoved a camera at Scooter, and within seconds Beau was sandwiched between heavily perfumed feminine flesh, those matching double D's pressing against his arms on each side of him.

"Say nitrous oxide," Scooter instructed.

"I thought it was cheese—isn't it cheese?" Tara asked.

On the other side of the camera, Scooter, ever the prankster, grinned.

"Cheese is fine," Beau assured her. He wasn't particularly surprised when one of them grabbed his ass a second later.

Scooter snapped the photo and returned the camera. Sherree murmured a thank-you and turned her attention back to Beau. "Want to party with us later?" she asked.

The invitation didn't surprise him any more than her copping a feel. Women liked him. They always had. And he liked them, too. And no doubt Tara and Sherree had a good time in mind and it was sort of crazy because it'd been a while since he'd *partied* and they were hot, but he just wasn't feeling it.

He shook his head. "Unfortunately, I've got a busy evening, ladies. No partying for me."

Sherree offered a moue of disappointment and another rub of her bodacious silicone tatas against his bicep. "Then you'll just have to call us for your celebration party when you win." She tucked a piece of paper into his jeans pocket, sliding her fingers suggestively along the edge of his pants.

"I'll keep that in mind."

They left, mouthing in unison "Call me" over their shoulders.

"Lucky bastard," Scooter muttered. They both knew he was just talking. Scooter had lost his wife, Emma Jean, two years ago and had never mentioned another woman. Scooter didn't say much, but Beau knew he missed her. Hell, they'd been married longer than the thirty-two years Beau had been alive.

A father and his young son, both wearing Stillwell Motors Racing T-shirts, came by for an autograph. They left and Beau and the crew spent a few minutes discussing setup adjustments for 10.5 qualifying the following day.

"You staying here tonight?" Scooter asked.

"Might as well." His major sponsor had shelled out the money for a sweet setup at the end of last year's winning season. They'd outfitted Stillwell Motors Racing with a toter home and race trailer that were both nicer than what he was living in now. But soon…

If he walked away with the 10.5 championship again this year, he'd have his money in place to build his house. Just as he'd promised his father before he died sixteen years ago, Beau had taken care of his mother and his sister. But it had been more than a deathbed promise.

Before he drank himself to death, Monroe Stillwell had bankrupted them and they'd lost everything— their home, cars, even their furniture. They'd been left with the clothes on their back, tattered pride and precious little else. As a teenager, Beau had vowed he'd never owe a red penny to anyone again. If he didn't owe, no one could come in and take what he considered his.

Between racing and his construction business, he'd made enough money to build his mother a house and set her up with a dress shop in downtown Dahlia. He was damn proud that his mother had turned Beverly's Closet into a thriving enterprise. He'd put Caitlyn through college and helped her find a job. Now it was his turn.

His cell phone buzzed at his side and he glanced at the caller ID—speaking of the devil. He let it go to voice mail. Scooter raised an eyebrow in inquiry.

"Caitlyn," Beau said. "Between her and that wedding planner, they're driving me bat-shit crazy."

"Why don't you just talk to the woman and get it over with?"

"She wants to know when I can start the remodel on Belle Terre. I haven't had time to get out there." Which suited him just fine. Everyone looked at Caitlyn's fiancé, Cash Vickers, and saw Nashville's newest rising star. Beau looked at Vickers and saw heartbreak for his sister.

He didn't like Vickers. He didn't think for a second the guy was good enough for his baby sister. To begin with, women were all over the guy, and he seemed to like them in return. Second, Beau had been most unimpressed when Cash had bought Belle Terre. It seemed like a extravagant, fiscally irresponsible move to him. Caitlyn had already been the victim of one financially irresponsible man— their father. She sure as hell didn't need a husband who spent money like water. And forbidding Caitlyn to marry Vickers would simply push her in his direction all the harder. Not to mention that his sister was old enough to do whatever she wanted to do. But Beau figured if he dragged his feet long enough, time would prove his rope and Vickers would hang himself.

"And that wedding planner needs to get a life. She's called me twice a day every day for two weeks."

He'd been legitimately busy the first week, but her nagging calls had irritated him to the point that this past week it had become a game to try and drive her as bat-shit crazy by avoiding her calls as she was driving him.

Scooter shook his head. "You might as well surrender now. Women and weddings. You ain't gonna know a minute's peace until they trade I-do's." He should know. His daughter, Carlotta, had gotten married the year before Emma Jean died.

"You never surrender until you've put up the good fight."

"I'm telling you, Beau, you might win a skirmish or two, but they'll win the war."

Beau grinned when he remembered the voice mail Ms. Natalie Bridges had left him earlier today. She'd been polite but he didn't miss the terse impatience underlying her message. She was frustrated. That was good. Maybe she'd quit and Caitlyn would have to start all over with another wedding planner. All of which meant more time for Vickers to screw up and show Caitlyn his true colors.

"I've got a couple of good battles left in me. Let Nightmare Natalie bring it on."

THERE IT WAS. Black toter home and trailer with Stillwell Motors Racing emblazoned on the side in purple and silver. Finally. Now that she'd rubbed a blister on her heel from hobbling along in a broken shoe.

Three men in uniforms that matched the black, silver and purple color scheme were under what should've been the hood of the car. Except the hood was sitting on a rack to the side. Whatever. She cleared her throat, interrupting.

"Excuse me. I'm looking for Beau Stillwell." She glanced expectantly from one man to the other. A short guy with thinning red hair had the name Scooter embroidered on his shirt. Next to him stood a lanky fellow with a crew cut, whose shirt designated him as Tim. On the left side of the car was an African-American named Darnell.

The short man exchanged a quick, almost imperceptible glance with the other two and stepped forward. "Scooter Lewis," he introduced himself. He grimaced and shook his head with a grin. "You'd probably rather not shake my hand right now."

"No problem. I'm Natalie Bridges and I'm—"

Scooter—she was so sure his mother hadn't given him that name at birth—interrupted with a nod and a quick grin. "You're that wedding planner out of Nashville."

Lanky Tim couldn't contain a snicker, which earned him an elbow in the side from Darnell. "Hey, man, watch it." Tim groused.

"Yes. I'm the wedding planner. It's so nice to meet you, Mr. Lewis." She tilted her chin up a notch while keeping her smile firmly in place. She didn't have to be the sharpest tool in the shed to figure out that if these three had heard of her it wasn't because their boss had been singing her praises.

"Just call me Scooter. Everybody does. And this here's Tim and Darnell."

"Gentlemen." She nodded and smiled a greeting while Tim shuffled his feet and blushed and Darnell bobbed his head in a quick acknowledgment. "I can see you're busy and I apologize for interrupting. If someone could just tell me where I might find Mr. Stillwell…" If they told her he'd just left the track, she wasn't so sure she wouldn't just pitch a hissy fit right here, right now.

Scooter jerked his thumb over his shoulder. "Beau's in the toter. I'd go get him for you, but…" He held up greasy hands. "Just let yourself in." Meltdown averted.

She skirted the car and gave a wide berth to a jack. She didn't know squat about cars, but even she recognized that was one big motor, which probably accounted for why Beau was the points leader. The overloud announcer had mentioned it exhaustively during her trek.

She stood on the lower step of the door Scooter had indicated and raised her hand to knock. "Just go on in," Scooter yelled, waving her on. "Don't worry about knocking. Folks come and go at the track all the time."

Okay. Far be it for her to screw up the way things

were done at the track. She grabbed the silver latch on the door that reminded her of her grandparents' camper and stepped into the motor home, clicking the door in place behind her. The similarities ended there. This certainly wasn't her grandparents' camper.

Instead of orange shag carpeting and yellowed Formica countertops, she was standing on hardwood flooring, looking at granite counter tops and a tiled backsplash. A baseball game, the sound muted, flickered on a flat-screen TV mounted over the opening to the cab's cockpit to her right. Dark, blackout curtains were drawn over the windows in the front, affording privacy inside.

And still no Beau Stillwell. "Hello?" she called out.

The panel door to her left slid open. Oh. My. All the spit in her mouth evaporated. A whoosh of heat roared through her as she stood rooted to the spot.

Tall. Big. Heavily muscled arms, chest, and legs. Dark hair on his head…and his chest…and his legs. Wet and naked, save for the white towel held precariously low on his hips. But it was the mocking blue eyes fringed with sooty lashes in a rugged, square-jawed face that did her in.

"Can I help you?"

"Are you Beau Stillwell?"

He bowed at the waist, overwhelmingly masculine, overwhelmingly arrogant, overwhelmingly almost naked. "At your service."

What she meant to say, what she fully planned to

say fell in the category of offering her name by way of introduction. But, honest to Bob, she couldn't even remember her name because just breathing the same air seemed to have annihilated all of her brain cells. Obviously. Because what came out of her mouth instead of a calm professional introduction was, "You can kiss my ass."

2

"THAT'S THE MOST interesting proposition I've heard all night," Beau said in a deliberate drawl despite the adrenaline rush that slammed him. He felt as if he'd been turned upside down just looking into her light brown eyes, which had widened with surprise and then narrowed with temper. He hung on to his cool…by a thread…because this woman shook him up…and he was never shaken up. "But maybe you could hop in the shower first to lose the beer smell." He moved the hand holding his towel in place, as if he were about to pass it to her. "You can borrow my towel."

She whipped around, presenting him with her back, before he got the last word out of his mouth. "Keep the towel," she snapped, staring straight ahead. Her rear view did nothing to settle him down. Beau liked his track straight and his women curvy, and she had nice curves from head to toe.

She drew a deep breath. "Look, I'm sorry. We got off on the wrong foot and I apologize for barging in. Mr. Lewis told me to just come on in without knocking."

"His idea of funny."

And she was his idea of hot.

Was that a snort?

"I'll step back out until you're decent," she said.

He itched to reach out and pull the pins from her hair and watch it tumble down around her shoulders. "No need to step outside. It'll take me no time to dress, but there's no guarantee I'll be decent. Clothes don't make the man."

She wanted to tell him to kiss her ass again. It was there in the rigid set of her shoulders. Instead she said, "Fine. I'll wait."

"I'll just be a minute," he paused for effect, "sweet thing." Beau slid the bathroom door closed and took two steps into the bedroom to "get decent." He was pretty sure the *sweet thing* business had been over the top. He'd sounded like a bona fide asshole. But that was the point—to goad her into quitting to delay the whole wedding thing. He'd told her to wait in the toter home because she was obviously uncomfortable with him being undressed, and the more uncomfortable she was the better. It didn't have a thing to do with some crazy-ass notion that now that he'd seen her he didn't want her to leave.

He pulled on fresh underwear and a pair of worn jeans. Natalie Bridges, he recognized her voice, was a wreck. He'd seen guys barrel-roll cars and climb out afterwards in better shape. But insanely he found her hot and sexy in a way he hadn't found the tube-top twins earlier.

Maybe it was the flash of anger in her brown eyes or the lush fullness of her pink lips or the semitumble of her hair. It was her mouth. There was something so damn sexy about the fact that with the rest of her obviously a mess—he was almost certain that was mustard on her left breast—her lipstick had been perfect. In fact, he was pretty damn sure she had the most perfect mouth he'd ever seen.

He tugged a black T-shirt over his head and tucked it into his jeans. She wasn't at all what he'd expected. He realized he'd sketched her in his head as thin, angular, rigid—a paragon of cool efficiency. But this woman was all curves, and she'd just blown a gasket with him.

If he pushed just a little harder, he'd have her right where he wanted her, so frustrated she'd toss in the towel and Caitlyn would be forced to start all over.

He hung his own wet towel on the hook outside the shower and slid open the door. She was still standing with her back to the bathroom.

"I'm as decent as I'm going to get. Now, what can I do for you, sweet thing?" Damn, he sounded obnoxious.

She pivoted to face him. Even with her mouth tightened like that, her lips were lush and full. "I'm Natalie Bridges," she said, extending her hand.

"Ah, Nightmare Natalie." He'd never been rude to a woman before, but he was doing a damn good job now. He took her hand to shake it, and it was as if a sparkplug had fired inside him. Her brown eyes widened but he wasn't sure whether it was because she felt the same surge or a reaction to the name he'd hung on her, or perhaps both.

She reclaimed her hand and totally threw him off track when she laughed, a husky, rich sound. "That's flattering…coming from Beau the Bastard."

He chuckled, thoroughly enjoying himself. "I've been called worse."

"No doubt." She smiled sweetly, and it had the same effect as when he hit the nitrous switch on his car and three G's slammed him back against the seat.

A brief knock sounded and then the door opened. Scooter, wearing an unrepentant grin, stuck his head in. "We're outta here." He nodded toward Nightmare Natalie. "Nice to meet you, Ms. Bridges."

"It was a pleasure, Mr. Lewis."

Ha. All three knew Scooter had set her up to walk in on him in the shower.

Scooter laughed. "Yes, ma'am. See ya in the morning, boss."

Scooter closed the door, once again shutting out the track noise and leaving them alone. She shifted awkwardly from one foot to the other, and he realized it was all the more awkward because she was missing the heel on one shoe.

"Have a seat, Miss Bridges. Or is it Mrs. Bridges?"

"Thank you," she said, perching primly on the edge of the couch. "And it's Miss. I'm not married."

"Here, let me help you out." He squatted in front of her and grasped the back of her left calf in his hand. She gasped and her muscle flexed against his palm. Her skin was warm and soft and he quelled the urge to stroke his hand along that tantalizing expanse from knee to ankle. Instead, lifting her leg in one hand, he plucked her shoe, the one with the heel still attached, off her foot. Her toenails were painted a similar shade of pink as her lips. Sexy.

"What are you doing?"

He stood. He placed the long, narrow heel on the counter with the rest of the shoe facing down. Beau slammed his hand down on the back, rendering her former stiletto a ballet slipper. He handed it back to her. "Now they match."

She quickly leaned forward and slipped the shoe back on, as if to preclude him from doing it. "Thank you…I think."

"You're welcome…I'm sure." He dropped to the sofa, more the size of a love seat, beside her, angling toward her and stretching out his legs. Deliberately invading her space and crowding her should definitely up his asshole quota.

"So, you're a wedding planner who's never been married? It seems it might limit your qualifications." He stretched his arm out along the back of the love seat. He was invading her space and conversely she was invading his. He was intensely aware those luscious lips of hers were ever so close, and all he had to do to release those hair pins was lean a bit to the right, raise his hand and pluck them out.

"Some professions don't require firsthand experience, Mr. Stillwell." He gave her points for standing her ground and not squirming closer to the kitchen counter. "Morticians. Brain surgeons. You know, that kind of thing. They manage just fine and so do I." She pulled a day planner out of her purse and opened it. It was a schedule and a neat script had pretty much every space filled in. She was a busy woman. "Now if we can just nail down some dates, I'll be more than happy to get out of your hair, Mr. Stillwell."

She obviously wanted to be anywhere other than in his company. That she wanted to leave, in and of itself, was something of a novel experience, except he had gone out of his way to be a jerk. Most of the time women were eager for his company. And while he'd been looking forward to watching some test and tune runs of the other drivers, he was actually having a damn good time needling the unorthodox and intriguingly unpredictable Ms. Bridges.

"Why don't we discuss it over dinner?"

"As appealing as that may be—" yet another kiss my ass "—I'm not particularly dressed for the occasion and as you so gallantly pointed out, I need a shower."

"The offer still stands to use my towel."

"Ever the gentleman, but I'll wait until I get home."

He'd been turned down. By Nightmare Natalie, no less.

"I JUST NEED a date when you'll have the remodel complete."

For God's sake, just give me a date so I can get the hell out of here. She was desperate, or maybe all the stress was getting to her and Beau Stillwell had just pushed her over the edge because he was arrogant and infuriating and the reason that a several-hundred-dollar outfit, shoes included, was now ruined, but some crazy, totally irrational part of her had wanted to accept his dinner invitation.

She had the oddest sense he was deliberately goading her. It was possible he was just an obnoxious jerk who went around calling women "sweet thing" and then insulting them in the next breath. There were plenty of sexist men who operated that way, but there'd been a flash of something in his blue eyes… And Natalie's foster-sister Shelby and Caitlyn Stillwell had roomed together in college. In all the time Natalie had known Caitlyn, which had been casually for almost five years, the younger woman might've been occasionally exasperated with her big brother, but there'd never been any doubt she respected him. It was difficult to imagine strong-minded Caitlyn respecting a jerk.

"How about a guesstimate," she prompted.

He shrugged those impossibly broad shoulders. "I can't give you a finish date until I get out to Belle Terre and see what has to be done."

"That makes sense." She nodded in agreement, trying to get along. "When are you available to do that?"

His eyes captured hers. Natalie found herself drowning in those blue depths. "When do *you* want to *do it?*"

A lazy, sensual spark in his eyes issued an invitation to wicked pleasure. A single, singeing look that tightened her nipples and dampened her panties.

She wet her lips with the tip of her tongue. Every thump of her heart seemed to echo *do it, do it, do it.* "Do it?"

"Yeah. When are you available?" His dark lashes formed a spiky frame for his eyes. She couldn't look away, couldn't think, could barely breathe.

"Available for what?"

Mocking amusement replaced sensual promise. "Try to keep up here, honey. When do you want to go out to Belle Terre with me to go over the remodel?"

Embarrassment flooded her. She'd prefer a hot poker in her eye. Actually, she'd prefer a hot poker up his ass. "I don't want to go out to Belle Terre with you. I don't need to be there. I just need to know a date you'll have it done."

"It'll go much faster if I have you there to explain exactly what Caitlyn wants done. And you can take notes for me."

"I know you have a secretary, Mr. Stillwell. I've spoken to her so often she's now on my Christmas-card list."

"Ah, but I need her in the office…to answer the phone."

Did he have any idea how busy she was? It was spring—high wedding season. Actually, the real question was did he care? And that answer was obviously *no*. "Fine. I'll make myself available to accommodate your busy schedule." Hopefully he wasn't impervious to sarcasm.

"How about Sunday, after the race?"

"No problem. As it happens, I don't have a wedding on schedule for Sunday. What time?"

"Probably around four. Just show up here and we'll go when I get through."

She managed not to gape at his total arrogance and disregard for her schedule. As if she had time to stand around cooling her heels at a racetrack while he indulged his testosterone-laden hobby. "I'll give you my cell number and you can just call me and I'll meet you out there."

"I'll try not to forget."

"I'll phone you to remind you."

"Sure. You've got my number." He all but smirked. They both knew how successful she'd been with him and the phone.

She gritted her teeth and mustered up a smile. If he was on some power trip and she had to kowtow to his schedule, then so be it. "I'll just come here. That way you won't forget."

"It's a date, then."

She tried to steadfastly ignore the way his voice seemed to caress the word *date,* but she couldn't stop her heart from beating faster.

"Yes. Four o'clock here on Sunday." Good. She had what she'd come for. An image of him still shower-damp and clad only in a towel flashed through her mind. Okay, she'd gotten more than she came for.

She jotted the time and notation in her day planner and stood. She hated to admit it, but it was much more comfortable with both the heels ripped off her poor shoes. "I'll see you then."

He stood, as well, dwarfing her in the close confines of the motor home. "Where'd you park?"

"The lot on the other side of the three-story building."

"Spectator parking. I'm heading up to the tower—" she assumed that was the three-story building "—to check on tomorrow's ladder. You can ride with me. It's a hike from here to spectator parking."

She wanted to turn him down but she was well aware of just how damn far it was. "Thank you. That'd be nice."

They both moved toward the door. "I'm a nice guy."

And she was Mary Poppins. "I'll take your word for it."

He reached past her to open the door, his shoulder brushing hers, his clean scent enveloping her. Her legs weren't quite steady as she walked down the two steps. Night had descended, but the racing continued. Cars were still being towed behind four-wheelers and golf carts. Across the pit "street," a crew was frantically working on a car under the glare of big floodlights mounted on stands.

He cupped his hand beneath her elbow and his touch sizzled right through her. "Okay, on you go. You might want to ride sidesaddle."

She looked from him to the four-wheeler he'd stopped beside and back to him. "You're going to take me on this?"

"Yeah. It's the best way to get around the track. Do you have an issue with four-wheelers?"

"No issue, I've just never been on one before." There'd never been money in her family for anything like a four-wheeler. And she'd never dated a guy with a four-wheeler—they weren't her type.

She caught a flash of his teeth. No doubt a mocking smile. "Ah. Your first time. I'll make sure you like it."

Did he have to make it sound like a seductive promise? Did her body, even knowing he was arrogant and manipulative and toying with her, have to respond with instant heat?

Make that a *yes* on both counts.

She stepped onto an open-grid platform and slid her butt to the back of the seat, keeping both her legs on one side and her knees pressed together. It wasn't so bad.

He climbed on in front of her, straddling the seat, presenting her with a solid wall of masculinity. He spoke over his shoulder, "You comfortable?"

Comfortable? With his absolute maleness crowding

her space? With his hip and leg pressed against hers? With her entire body humming at the proximity?

"Absolutely. Never more comfortable."

He cranked it. Not only was the engine loud, but she felt its vibration through her seat, which was strange, inappropriately erotic under the circumstances.

"You'll want to hold on," he said as he rolled to the edge of the pit road and looked both ways to see if the coast was clear. She lightly put one hand at his waist. The less body contact, the better.

One minute they were sitting there idling, the next they were off like a bat out of hell. She instantly, automatically wrapped both arms around him, hanging on for dear life.

"Woo!"

She heard his yell above the din and the rush of blood in her ears. Once she realized they weren't going to die, she had to admit she rather liked it—the rush of wind past them, the thrill of going fast. And, heaven help her, the feel of *him*.

Her right cheek and breast pressed against his back. She felt the play of muscles beneath the cotton T-shirt as he drove. Likewise, there was no mistaking the six-pack ripple of his belly beneath her clasped hands. He felt even better than he'd looked wearing that towel—and that was saying something.

She had the craziest, hormone-fueled desire to nuzzle the muscled expanse of his back, to slide her hands beneath the edge of his T-shirt and explore the hard ridges of his belly…and lower. Natalie's bad-girl side had the urge to experience skin on skin with Beau the Bastard.

He made a quick left, ground to a stop and killed the engine. He climbed off. He'd parked in the area chock-full of other four-wheelers and golf carts between the bleacher entrance and the tower. The starting line was right ahead of them, on the other side of the fence.

He reached for her and his hand engulfed hers as he helped her off. Much as she'd have liked to shrug off his assistance, her legs felt like rubber.

"Do you always drive like a maniac?" She tugged her hand free of his, determined to regain her equilibrium, which had seemed to fly out the window during the ride. It had to be his driving and not the fact that she'd been reduced to jelly legs from being wrapped around him. From wanting to stay wrapped around him. Dangerous ground, that.

He laughed. "A maniac?" He shook his head in pretend consternation, his blue eyes glittering. "Now that's disappointing. Since it was your first time, I gave you the slow ride. I'll try harder next time to make it better for you. By the way…" He reached out and casually brushed a hank of hair out of her eyes— her chignon was seriously destroyed at this point— as if he were a lover with every right to do so. His fingers barely grazed her skin but his touch echoed through her. "Two suggestions for Sunday. You might want to dress down a bit and you might want to lay off the beer."

He pivoted on his heel and strolled away, leaving her standing there.

She hated Beau Stillwell.

3

ON SUNDAY AFTERNOON, once she left Nashville behind on her way out to Dahlia, Natalie powered down her windows and let the wind blow through the van as she drove the twisting, turning back roads through the Tennessee hills. She could've taken the expressway route she'd opted for on Friday night but this was so much nicer. It reminded her of the drive out to her parents' farm. How could anyone be alive and not love springtime here?

She cranked the CD player, singing along with Seal to "Kiss from a Rose," when her cell phone rang. She didn't recognize the number but she turned down the volume and answered. Being available came with the job.

"Natalie Bridges."

"Are you coming?"

No salutation, no identification, no nothing, just that husky-voiced question in her ear. Beau Stillwell. She didn't even have to close her eyes—which was a good thing, considering she was driving—to imagine that voice in her ear asking that very question in very intimate circumstances. It was that kind of voice and he was that kind of man.

"I'm almost there." Dear God, what was wrong with her? She'd answered him on a matching husky note that implied intimacy when she'd meant to use her normal, efficient, brisk tone.

There was a long pause and her skin felt too warm even with the breeze blowing through the windows. He finally spoke. "Good. We're about to go to the finals. I'll send Scooter to pick you up on the four-wheeler. What are you driving?"

She cringed. She didn't want to tell him. Most of the time she didn't care. Sure, she'd like a sexy little European sportscar—she practically drooled every time she saw an Audi roadster—but that wasn't practical in her business. Practical had been buying the family vehicle from her folks at a deep discount. It was nice enough, but this was a man who was all about fast cars, and hers was anything but. She patted the steering wheel by way of silent apology to her mobile workhorse.

"It's a silver minivan."

He laughed—the son of a bitch actually laughed—in her ear.

"You try hauling a wedding dress or a wedding cake in anything smaller."

"I guess that's true enough. I'll tell Scooter to look for a silver minivan."

He disconnected the call before she had time to

respond. She returned her cell phone to the center console. "Bite me," she muttered as she turned the volume on he CD player back up.

She would not let him get to her today the way he had Friday night. She cringed inside every time she remembered telling him to kiss her ass. She'd suffered a severe case of temporary insanity due to extenuating circumstances but she'd make sure it wasn't repeated.

Friday night had been weird all the way around. She'd seen men in bathing suits, underwear—she'd even seen a couple of them naked. So what was the big deal about Mr. Stillwell draped in a towel?

Maybe because he was ripped and gorgeous…if a woman found that combination of muscle, black hair, intense blue eyes, a slightly wicked grin and a faint scar across the perfection of his left cheek appealing. Her assistant, Cynthia, would do backflips over him. Because he was Cynthia's type. He was not, however, Natalie's type. Natalie preferred her men more polished and urbane. Therefore she put it down to the total weirdness of the night and that from the instant she'd laid eyes on Beau Stillwell's near nakedness a minivolcano had sprung to life inside her. She'd felt hot, flushed, unsettled.

She turned left at a sign with an arrow indicating Dahlia Speedway. Even a shower and a small glass of chardonnay hadn't settled her down on Friday night. Despite the fact that she'd gone to bed mentally reviewing her checklist for the Morris-Pitchford wedding the following day, the same as she always did the night before an event, he had plagued her in her dreams. Crazy dreams.

She was directing a rehearsal and then the dinner and somehow it became the wedding itself, and just when things were going smoothly, Beau Stillwell would appear with his mocking grin and Natalie would look down and discover she was only wearing a towel. She'd hurry and find her clothes and put herself back together, only to have Beelzebub Stillwell reappear, and once again she was appalled to find her clothes gone and a towel about her sarongwise.

She'd woken up tired and out of sorts, and she'd nearly left the last-minute sewing kit behind on her way out the door to the pre-wedding photo shoot. All *his* fault.

And this morning? She'd tried on at least five different outfits until she'd finally settled on a fitted cotton-spandex apricot T-shirt layered beneath a short green jacket with wide-legged jeans and wedge heels. Casual but still professional. This was, after all, work and not a social engagement. And then she'd dithered—might as well call it the way it was—over whether to pull her hair up in a ponytail, or her work chignon, or leave it down. The chignon seemed too fussy, the ponytail too girlish. In the end she'd left it hanging loose over her shoulders and down her back.

Natalie had no delusions about what she looked

like. She wasn't traffic-stopping beautiful and she needed to lose ten…okay, fifteen, maybe twenty… pounds. She was average. Average height. Average overweight. Run-of-the-mill brown eyes. But her one point of vanity was her hair. She'd been blessed with good hair. It was long and thick with just enough curl to give it body.

All told, it had taken her far too long to get ready but it was absolutely *not* because she was concerned about what Beau Stillwell thought of her appearance. No. She couldn't give a fig whether he found her attractive or not. She was not trying to compensate for having given a general first impression of a walking, talking disaster.

She stopped at the gate and flashed the ticket she'd bought Friday evening. Before she'd put the minivan in Park in the far corner of the crowded lot—there were lots of people here today—Scooter pulled up in front of her van.

"Nice to see you again, Ms. Bridges. Climb on the back." He grinned. "You're just in time to see Beau open a can of whup-ass."

"I can hardly wait." Despite her sarcasm, she returned his grin.

He handed her a blue wrist band. "Put this on."

Natalie complied but asked all the same, "What is it?"

"It shows you're a pit crew member. C'mon, let's go race."

Whatever. She'd only shown up to make sure Mr. Stillwell didn't conveniently "forget" their appointment. However, if being a pit crew member was what it took to drag his butt out to Belle Terre, then she was pit-crewing.

She shrugged and climbed up on the four-wheeler behind Scooter. Today she wasn't riding sidesaddle, and instead of wrapping her arms around his waist, she merely held on to the rack that fanned out over the rear fenders. Hmm. In retrospect she could've held on to that rack on Friday night, too. Oh, well.

"You settled?" Scooter asked over his shoulder.

"Yes, sir." Even though he'd sent her in the toter home the other night knowing good and well she'd probably find Beau in some state of undress, she liked Scooter Lewis. With his freckled face and dancing eyes, he reminded her of a mischievous elf.

They took off with a roar, but instead of going to the left in the direction of the pits, Scooter drove into an eight-lane asphalted area where cars, some still attached to tow ropes, were lined up one behind the other and drivers milled about. At the front, the cars converged into two openings and then rolled forward for their turn down the track.

"Staging lanes," he yelled over his shoulder.

She nodded in return. Staging lanes. Okay. Whatever that exactly was, she wasn't sure, but it was loud and noisy…and kind of exciting. Above the din of car engines and male voices, the announcer sounded like a circus barker. "Get ready for some driving, folks. It's the event you've been waiting for—the bad boys of outlaw racing, 10.5's Beau Stillwell and Jason Mitchell taking it head-to-head down the track. Nitrous versus turbo in the final round."

Scooter pulled up next to the black and purple Camaro and she climbed off the four-wheeler. Every inch of her was aware of Beau Stillwell, but she deliberately looked at and spoke to his crew members, Darnell and Tim, first. A whoosh of red ran up Tim's face at her hello. He was obviously one of those guys more at ease around a fan belt than a female.

Finally, she turned to face Beau Stillwell. He wore a half-cocked smile but it was the lazy sweep of those bright blue eyes framed in dark lashes down and back up her that sucked the breath from her and sent her mind skittering to naughty places. "You clean up nice, Ms. Bridges." He leaned down and for one heart-stopping, pulse-pounding moment she was certain he was going to kiss her. There was a lambent sensuality in his eyes, in the way he bent his head. Her whole body tingled in anticipation. The air between them seemed to crackle.

He canted his head to the left, his dark hair teasing against her cheek, and sniffed delicately. She could almost feel the faint scrape of his five-o'clock shadow against her neck. She was on the verge of spontaneous combustion. He straightened. "You smell a whole lot better, too."

He smirked and she wanted to do something awful to him. Instead she smiled sweetly. "You smell terrible."

Okay. Not the wittiest comeback in the world, but good lord, he'd paralyzed over half her brain cells when he'd leaned in close that way. Her heart was still tap-dancing against her ribs. It was the best she could do on short notice and short-circuit.

"You're not into eau de oil and sweat?"

"Afraid not."

Tim, she could've kissed him, chose that moment to interrupt. "I brought the tires down to ten and quarter and heated the bottles to nine-hundred." He handed Beau a jacket, which he shrugged into.

Beau zipped up the jacket. "Good deal." He reached into the open door of the car and took out a black neck brace and snapped it into place. He pulled on a helmet, buckling the chinstrap, leaving the visor up. Unfairly, he was even more gorgeous in a helmet. Last was a pair of black, heavy gloves.

Natalie had never been much of a uniform woman. Cynthia, her assistant, got all hot and bothered by firefighters, cops and soldiers. She said the uniform did it for her. Icing on top of a male cupcake. Natalie had always favored a man in a suit and tie, but Beau was all suited up in racing gear and looked sexy and hot, and it was even more galling that he was the one who was flipping her switch.

He folded himself into the car, sliding between

foam-covered bars that formed a cage inside. "Wish me luck," he said with a flash of a smile.

While she'd wanted to do him bodily harm two minutes ago when he'd left her feeling like a fool, she quite suddenly realized that all that safety gear was in place for a reason. Even though he was annoying and infuriating and generally rubbed her the wrong way, she wanted the arrogant bastard to win safely. She *was* wearing his pit crew band, after all.

"Good luck."

"When it's a pretty woman doing the send-off, it's customary to offer the driver a good-luck kiss."

His gaze lingered on her mouth. That look in his eyes and the very thought of kissing him weakened her knees and sent a bolt of heat through her. "I'll pass."

"Too bad." He winked at her and clicked his visor down into place.

Tim leaned in, fastened a heavy-gauged "net" over the window opening and slammed the driver door shut.

Darnell handed her what looked like an old-fashioned headset. "Put these on. They're ear protection. It's about to get loud."

She put the headset on and she could still hear, but everything was muffled. The car roared to life and she was glad to have the protection, because even with it, the sound was loud enough to vibrate through her body.

Inside the car, Beau sat with his hands gripping the wheel, staring straight ahead.

"He's going through the run in his head, visualizing it," Darnell said, next to her.

She nodded to let him know she'd heard.

The rest happened fast. She and Darnell rode the four-wheeler up to an area closer to the starting line, on the other side of the low wall that separated the track from the stands. Spectators packed the stands. The crowd's excitement was a nearly palpable thing. She knew how they felt. From the moment Tim had slammed the door and Beau had started the car, she'd been revved up inside.

Tim was out between the two cars with a video camera but Darnell stayed with her on the four-wheeler and explained what was happening as Beau "smoked" the tires in the burnout box, which was essentially standing on the brake and the gas at the same time. This created a cloud of choking tire dust but heated up the slick tires so they'd stick to the asphalt track. Scooter then stood in front of the car, giving hand signals, directing Beau left or right, lining the car up "in the groove," where the tires would have the best chance of gripping.

A final tap on the hood by Scooter, a sharp nod of acknowledgment from Beau and he rolled the car forward until the yellow bulb on "the tree"—the staging sequence of red, yellow, green bulbs in the middle of the starting line between the two cars—lit up. Then the roar really became deafening as both drivers revved their engines. The lights changed and they were off. Fast. Furious. For a second it looked as if the driver racing in the other lane was going to swerve into Beau's lane and Natalie thought her heart might very well stop.

And then it was over. Darnell pumped his hand in the air and yelled, pointing at the signs flanking the end of the track. The sign on Beau's side had a lit bulb over the top, designating him the winner, and below it a display of 4.192, 184.92.

Even she could figure it out. 185 miles per hour in 4.40 seconds.

Damn right that was fast, stupid ass.

BEAU TOSSED the wet towel onto the bathroom floor. Tim would clean the toter home up when Scooter got it back to his place. Such was the lot of the gofer on a crew. Such had been Beau's lot when he'd first started out in racing many moons ago, when he was the gofer and his dad was the one climbing behind the wheel of a race car.

He retreated to the bedroom and took his own sweet time dressing. He pushed aside a twinge of remorse. He'd been wasting Natalie's time for a full hour and a half now. After the tow back to the pits, the Horsepower TV reporter had conducted a quick interview and then fellow racers and fans alike had swarmed them. The racers offered congratulations. Most of the fans wanted autographs and a picture with Beau and the car.

Natalie had stood by quietly, out of the way, but those big brown eyes of hers hadn't missed a thing. The tube-top duo from Friday night, Sherree and Tara, had shown up again with a celebration offer. Ms. Bridges had merely quirked an amused eyebrow in his direction and a faint look of disdain, as if they were all somewhat distasteful.

And the whole time he'd been thinking about the way she'd smelled when he'd leaned into her neck before the race. The tickle of her hair against his cheek. The curve of her sexy, sexy mouth. And the crazy, out-of-control feeling she stirred in him.

He squashed any guilt at wasting her time. Given a choice between wasting her time or sitting by while his sister made a mistake marrying Cash Vickers… Well, there was really no question which was more important.

All told, he thought his plan was working okay. He just needed to watch himself, because in the staging lanes, for a second, when he was teasing her, deliberately letting her think he was about to kiss her, he damn near had. She had the most luscious, inviting mouth, with a full lower lip and a cute bow for the top one.

He sauntered back outside and found the enemy consorting with his troops in the small lounge in the front of the race trailer. She was laughing at something Scooter had said, some crazy bullshit no doubt, and his body tightened as the musical notes seemed to dance through the air. Her smile stiffened when she noticed him in the doorway. Good. That was what he wanted, wasn't it?

"Ready?"

She nodded, her chestnut-brown hair moving over her shoulders in a gut-clenching sensual slide. "I just need a ride back to my car."

"Leave your car and we'll pick it up on the way back. We've got to come this way anyway."

Tim spoke up. "You can ride up front with Scooter, if'n you want to," he offered, a flush of red whooshing from his neck to the top of his crew cut before he even finished the sentence. Scooter always drove the rig and the passenger seat was a place of honor, sort of a gimme, for Tim, who mostly handled the grunt work. And now the grunt was willingly giving up that honor. Tim seemed to have developed a crush.

A small frown furrowed her brow as she glanced from Tim to Beau, obviously confused, and equally reluctant to hurt Tim's feelings by turning down his offer. "Ride with Scooter? We're all going to Belle Terre?"

"No, ma'am," Darnell said. "We're all going to Headlights."

"Headlights? What is Headlights and what happened to Belle Terre?"

"Headlights is the ice house and local watering hole between here and Dahlia." Darnell shot Beau a chastising look. "We usually stop off for dinner at the end of a race weekend."

Another chastising look—this one from *her.* "You didn't mention dinner."

All part of his plan. Beau shrugged. "I forgot. We'll head on out to Belle Terre after we eat."

Scooter snorted. "C'mon and ride with me. And dinner's on us."

She deliberately turned her back to Beau, presenting him with a view of her well-rounded bottom, and beamed a smile at the other three. "Charming companions and a free meal. How can I turn down that offer?"

A quarter hour later, they were seated at the number nine picnic table, the number painted on each end in fluorescent orange, after much backslapping and high fives as they made their way across the peanut-hull-littered concrete floor in the noisy din that was Headlights after a race. No matter how crowded it was, however, Jeb Worth always held the number nine for the Stillwell crew. It was a long-standing tradition. Beau wound up sitting next to the Nightmare.

"What do you think of Headlights?" he asked. She didn't strike him as an ice house kind of gal.

"So far, so good. The music's loud." She said it as if it were a bonus. "If the beer's cold and the fries are greasy, we're in business."

Sandy Larabie, her tongue as acid as her heart was big, showed up to take their order, a doe-eyed girl in tow. "This is Gina. She's in training, so you behave." Sandy shot Scooter a steely-eyed glare. Scooter lived to aggravate Sandy. Actually, Scooter lived for mischief in general. "A root beer for Junior," Sandy told Gina, jerking her head in Tim's direction. Sandy referred to anyone under legal drinking age as Junior. "And a pitcher of what for the rest of you?"

"Bud Light. We won." Scooter smirked.

"Three or four mugs?" She eyed Natalie in question.

"Four." Natalie didn't hesitate.

"I would've pegged you for a white wine drinker," Beau said.

"I would've pegged you for a mullet." Ha. He'd never gone in for the longer-in-the-back hairstyle. "I guess we were both wrong."

"What exactly happened to you the other night?" Scooter asked.

She laughed, shaking her head, and it struck Beau as ball-tightening sexy. He had no problem imagining her on top of him, shaking her head just that way. "I got distracted by the T-shirt display about the same time my heel wedged in a crack in the asphalt, which led to an accident with a guy and his beer and hot dog."

Scooter made a sympathetic clicking sound. "Did it ruin everything?"

"Pretty much. The skirt made it through."

"You know Caitlyn and Beau's ma, Beverly, has a right nice shop there in the square in Dahlia. Drop in sometime and let her fix you up. We'll cover the bill."

Had Scooter lost his mind? "The hell you say," Beau said.

Scooter fixed him with an unyielding eye. "She

wouldn't have been at the track if she hadn't been looking for you."

The Nightmare couldn't contain a little smirk in Beau's direction.

"It's not my fault she's clumsy," he said, deliberately goading her. There was a tantalizing sway to her hips when she walked, but it damn sure couldn't be classified as clumsy.

She narrowed her brown eyes. "I am not clumsy."

The trainee delivered the beer and Tim's root beer. Darnell poured and they all hoisted their mugs in a toast. "To another win…and many more to come," Scooter said.

The wash of beer was bust-your-kneecaps cold going down. Beau settled his mug on the table. He'd nurse the rest of it through dinner. He knew he wasn't the man his father had been, but Beau always held himself to a one-drink limit.

Tim unfolded his lanky length from the picnic table, muttered an excuse-me and headed to the jukebox. Scooter groaned and Darnell rolled his eyes. The Nightmare looked at Beau, a question in her brown eyes. "Prepare yourself for a Kenny Chesney miniconcert."

She laughed, her mouth curving in an easy smile and for a second he felt damn near light-headed. He shook his head slightly. Maybe he'd just skip the rest of his beer.

"I like Kenny Chesney."

"So did we…the first hundred times we heard him," Darnell said in a mournful drawl.

"Could be worse," Scooter said. "Could be Cash Vickers we was listening to. Ain't that right, Beau?"

Beau shrugged and he felt the woman next to him eyeing him in inquiry. He deliberately didn't look her way. Not that it was a state secret, but damn it'd be nice if Scooter could just hold his tongue and not stir shit up.

"You're not a Cash Vickers fan?"

Caitlyn hadn't known Cash nearly long enough. And Beau wasn't certain that Cash was good enough for his baby sister.

"Not particularly, no," Beau said. Let her make what she wanted to of that.

Sandy and Gina showed up bearing five red, paper-lined baskets loaded with burgers and fries. "Y'all need anything else?"

"We're good."

Beau tucked into his burger. Lunch had been a long time ago.

"Would you pass the catsup, Mr. Stillwell?"

"Sure thing, Ms. Bridges."

Scooter shook his head. "You can't sit down and have burgers and beers and still be Mr. Stillwell and Ms. Bridges. Nat'lie, meet Beau. Beau, this here's Nat'lie."

Beau passed the tomato-emblazoned bottle. "There you are, Natalie."

"Thank you, Beau."

Damn, that sent a little shiver through him.

"That wasn't so hard, was it?" Scooter said.

"Almost painless," the little smart-ass shot back, upending half the bottle in a corner of her basket.

Alex Morgan and "Black Jack" Riley stopped at the edge of their table, Jack's arm slung around Alex's shoulder, staking his claim.

"Nice finish today," Alex said, with a quick nod of her blond head, "You must've changed your setup."

"Yeah, we changed the heads this week," Darnell said. "It's the best sixty-foot we've had."

Darnell was talking but there was no disguising Alex's frank curiosity about Natalie. And Beau had been deliberately obnoxious but he couldn't totally abandon the manners his mother had drilled into him.

"Natalie, meet Alex Morgan and Jack Riley. Alex is one of the best mechanics in Dahlia. She owns the garage out at the track and another one in town with her dad. They're partners. Jack's from your neck of the woods. He's a DEA agent out of Nashville." He looked at the couple. "Natalie's a wedding planner. She's working with Caitlyn on the big event."

The pleased-to-meet-you's went around, and from Alex's look she clearly speculated why his baby sister's wedding planner was kicking back post-race with him and his crew. In fact, she rather pointedly glanced from Natalie to Beau and back again, silently asking if they were an item.

Sharp-eyed Natalie didn't miss the unspoken question. She wrinkled her elegant little nose, almost as if she'd caught a whiff of a bad smell. "Uh, no. Certainly not that." Hmph. That she'd be so damn lucky. He could name half a dozen women, round that up to an even dozen, who'd like to be sitting right where she was parked now. She didn't need to look as if he were something scraped from the bottom of the barrel. "Mr. Stillwell...I mean, Beau, is a hard man to get in touch with. My job title is wedding planner but sometimes that involves being a tracker—"

"Stalker," he interjected under his breath, garnering a laugh from everyone except the accused, who slanted him the evil eye.

"—and a babysitter."

"Warden," he corrected. "We're heading out to Belle Terre after this to figure out the remodel schedule for the wedding."

Jack squeezed Alex's shoulders. "You might want to hook up with her," he said to the petite blonde, and then looked at Natalie. "I'm trying to talk her into getting married before the end of the year, but she says she doesn't have time to get it together. I'm thinking you could help make this happen."

"Absolutely." Quicker than the staging lights rundown she had two business cards in her hand and was passing them across the table, one to Jack and one to Alex. "I can handle as much or as little as you want me to. Give me a call or send me an e-mail and we'll talk about what you want."

"We'll let y'all get back to your supper, and I don't want to hold you up from getting out to Belle Terre. Just wanted to say congrats on the win." Alex tucked the card into the top pocket of her denim overalls. "I'll give you a call next week."

Natalie beamed a megawatt smile at her potential client. "I'll be looking forward to it."

Alex and Black Jack were barely out of earshot when Scooter started filling Natalie in on Jack posing as a driver to uncover a drug ring and the whole mess that followed. Even Darnell chimed in with the skinny on Alex growing up a motherless tomboy. Beau knew it was all over when Tim screwed up his courage to relate how Jack and Alex had fallen in love.

What was wrong with this damn picture? He'd dragged her out to the track and along to dinner to tie up her time and frustrate her. He'd figured she'd hate the raucousness of Headlights. The whole plan was to push her buttons until she tossed in the wedding planner towel and quit on Caitlyn. Instead, she was swilling beer and chowing down on burgers, holding court with his guys and charming her way into picking up new clients.

This was just damn wrong on so many levels. It was definitely time to step things up a notch.

4

NATALIE WALKED OUT of Headlights into the relative quiet of the crowded parking lot, surrounded by her new friends, Scooter, Darnell and Tim. They were all sweetie pies. The thorn in her side had stopped to talk to the restaurant owner—she thought he'd introduced him as Jeb—on the way out.

"Looks like y'all are gonna run out of daylight," Scooter said.

True enough, the day had begun to soften around the edges, making way for a Tennessee spring evening. Already, a sliver of a moon was showing itself in the sky. That was okay. Afternoon, evening or night, it didn't matter. She was determined they'd get this done.

"It'll be fine." She patted her purse, "I brought my flashlight."

"Smart thinking," Darnell said in his quiet, reflective way as they crossed the gravel lot to where the big outfit took up several parking spots. Of course, Stillwell Motors Racing wasn't alone. Half a dozen race trailers commandeered spots.

Natalie checked her watch. Nearly seven o'clock. "We'll definitely need a flashlight at this rate. Does he have any concept of time?" Was it her imagination or did Scooter and Darnell exchange a look? "What?"

"I didn't say anything," Darnell said.

"I didn't say nuthin', neither," Scooter seconded.

While Darnell and Scooter looked guilty, Tim appeared confused. "Beau's always on time, for everything."

"Really?"

"Yes, ma'am. He's amazing. I keep the log book on all of our runs but I don't really need to. He can tell you what the track temperature was and our setup from three races ago. Beats anything I've ever seen."

"Wow. That is pretty amazing." Uh-huh. And he didn't like Cash Vickers. This was getting more and more interesting. "Sounds like he has a heck of a memory, too."

Tim nodded, reminding her of one of those bobble-head dolls. "I keep telling him he oughta go on one of those game shows. He'd win, for sure."

"Tim, whyn't you go check the tire pressure on the trailer tires?" Scooter suggested. "It'd be bad to have a blowout on the way home."

"Yes, sir." He ambled off to the rear of the trailer.

Scooter lowered his voice. "You can't pay Tim no never mind. His daddy went to county jail last year and since then Beau's really taken him under his wing. Tim sorta idolizes him."

She refused to feel all warm and gooey inside because Beau had mentored a kid. She absolutely was not going to add a gold star to the top of the heap of attraction that was simmering inside her. Sitting next to him at dinner… "That's sad."

"Which part?" Darnell asked. As far as she could tell, Darnell didn't miss much.

"Both."

Beau, the man of many faces, crossed the parking lot, his long legs eating up the distance. Her pulse began to race as he closed the gap. "I'm ready if you are. We're burning daylight."

He made it sound as if he'd been standing around waiting on *her.* She ground her teeth and resisted the urge to thwack him upside his too-handsome head with her purse. "I've been ready." Generally speaking, for the last two weeks. Specific to today, since four o'clock.

She bid the other guys goodbye and this time headed toward Beau's truck. Funny, but she thought he'd hesitated for a second before walking around to his side, as if he was going to open her door for her and reconsidered at the last minute. She was finding herself more and more intrigued with exactly who and what Beau Stillwell was.

She climbed into the truck, settled against the tweed upholstered seat and buckled up. The floorboard was a utilitarian, uncarpeted vinyl. A worn aluminum clipboard sat in the center of the bench seat along with an orange measuring tape. While it was neat and clean, the truck obviously had both miles and years on it. "I'd have put you in a Corvette, Camaro or Mustang," she said.

"Have you ever tried hauling two-by-fours in one of those?" He turned the key and started the truck.

"Guess that wouldn't work out too well," she said. "Why does your engine sound funny?"

He hung a left out of the parking lot onto the highway. "It's a diesel." He patted the dashboard, "She's a workhorse."

They rolled along and silence filled the space between them. She noted his hands on the steering wheel. He had broad, square hands with a smattering of dark hair on them. His nails were short and clean. They were the capable, masculine hands of a working man and they suited the hard-muscled rest of him that she'd seen. A warm flush spread through her. She could almost guarantee they'd be callused and rasp against a woman's skin—more specifically, her skin.

Natalie was abruptly achingly aware that only about a foot separated them. How was it that he always seemed to invade her space when she was around him?

And what in the heck was wrong with her? She'd spent two weeks tracking him down to sit idly by and contemplate his hands? Not hardly.

She opened her day planner and flipped to her notes detailing the particulars of the Stillwell-Vickers wedding. "Caitlyn's discussed with you what she wants done at Belle Terre?"

"As my granddaddy used to say, is the backside of a pig pork?" He slanted a sideways glance her direction. "If you know my baby sister at all, you'll know she has no problem telling someone what she wants and when she wants it." Evident affection underscored his wry exasperation.

Natalie chuckled. The few times Natalie had been around the pretty little blonde, when her sister, Shelby, had roomed with her at the Watkins College of Art and Design, Caitlyn had always been forthcoming and occasionally demanding. However, she didn't strike Natalie as spoiled so much as indulged—a subtle, yet important difference. "Yeah. I guess that's true."

"Right. You've worked with her on the wedding."

"And I met her a couple of times when she and Shelby were roomies. Have you ever met Shelby?" Her baby sister had mentioned Caitlyn's older brother occasionally. She mostly just groused that he was more of a father than a brother and complained about him being overprotective.

"No. I've heard plenty about her from Caitlyn but I've never met her. I keep a busy schedule." A flick of his blue eyes in her direction set her heart beating a little faster. "Is she as pretty as you are?"

All her breath lodged in her chest. He thought she was pretty? She'd always been the practical one, the smart one, the organized one, but out of a long-running list of foster sisters, she'd never been described as the pretty one. She curled her fingers into her palm.

And this wasn't about her. He'd asked about Shelby, even if it had been in context with Natalie. Shelby and Beau Stillwell? Over her dead body. Beau Stillwell had heartbreaker written all over him. "She's too young for you."

"How old do you think I am?"

She'd guess early thirties. Chronologically he wasn't so far out of bounds. Experiencewise, however… And it wasn't simply because Natalie felt as if she'd been caught in a deep current of desire and was being swept along that every part of her rebelled at the thought of her foster sister dating him.

She was her parents' only biological child, but she maintained the role of oldest child rather than only child because her parents had started fostering children when Natalie was five. Even as a child she'd been the one to try to bring some semblance of organization to their household. Her hippies-at-heart parents had never figured out that having structure was liberating rather than confining.

All her big sister instincts rose to the surface. She didn't think Beau was actually interested in Shelby but just in case… "Too old for my little sister."

He offered a challenging smile that sizzled through her nonetheless. "You don't like me, do you, Natalie?"

No. *Like* wasn't a word she associated with him.

It was as if he bypassed every reasonable, rational, functional aspect of her and tapped into her elemental core. When she was around him, she felt everything with a new intensity. It was as if she were supercharged. She'd never been so aware of herself as a woman and him as a man. But did she like him? Did she particularly like feeling this way? No. But then again, it was a rhetorical question. "That's really immaterial, isn't it?"

"I don't see it that way. We're going to be working closely together on the remodel."

Working closely with him on anything struck her as a lousy idea. He turned everything in her world topsy-turvy and Natalie didn't like topsy-turvy. "Once we get the dates down, it really doesn't have anything to do with me."

"That's not the way Caitlyn sees it." He looked altogether too smug. "She said that's what she was paying you for." His voice dropped and slid over her like the play of velvet against naked flesh. "She assured me you'd be at my beck and call."

Her. Him.

Naked. Needy.

Wet. Hot.

Beck and call.

The very idea sent a shiver down her spine and a rush of slick heat between her thighs.

"Within reason," she managed to say.

"Reason's not part of the deal."

WHAT THE HELL? He liked women. He liked spending time with women, but he *never* got caught up in them. But that's exactly how he felt about Natalie Bridges. Caught up. Tangled. Intrigued.

Interested…aroused, even…was fine, but that wasn't what all of this was about, he reminded himself. Caitlyn was going to make a big mistake and it was up to him to make sure she didn't, by whatever means possible.

Beau rounded the last curve beneath the arch of overhanging oaks and Belle Terre spread before him. Son of a bitch. Cash Vickers would have to show up with a harem and light a crack pipe to get his baby sister to walk away from this.

Set on prime rolling Tennessee hills, even with its vague air of neglect reflected in sagging and missing shutters, Belle Terre was spectacular. The house itself boasted an imposing front of soaring columns and two stories of floor-to-ceiling windows with a second-story balcony overlooking the front door.

"That's a helluva tax write-off, wouldn't you say?" he said.

Natalie pushed her hair back over her shoulder. Thick and shiny, it was the kind of hair that left a man itching to run his fingers through it—or hungry to feel it teasing against his bare chest, his belly and finally his thighs as it followed the trail blazed by her lush mouth over his body. She quirked an eyebrow in inquiry. "You haven't seen Belle Terre before? Not even the video?"

He pushed aside a ripple of guilt. Videographer was Caityln's professional calling, but it wasn't his deal. "Nope. I don't spend a lot of time watching music videos." Apparently the video—Caitlyn's project and her intro to Cash Vickers—that went with his hit song "Homesick" had been shot at Belle Terre. According to Caitlyn, Vickers had bought the place because she'd fallen in love with it. "First I heard of it was when he gave her Belle Terre and a ring. I've been meaning to get out here but I've been busy."

He glanced over at her. The dying sunlight slanting in through her window picked out red threads in her hair.

"You know, Caitlyn has her heart set on having the wedding here," she said.

He had the oddest feeling that they could have been discussing their own child, years from now. It was the first time he'd ever felt someone really understood the level of responsibility he felt for Caitlyn. "I caught that."

"Then it's a good thing we're sequencing out the remodel today. It's a bit of a tight timeline."

Yeah, if they were actually looking at an August wedding. And he caught on right away that she was taking him to task. He was quick that way.

He parked in the circular driveway that fronted the stately columned home. "My sister is obsessed with

Gone with the Wind." He didn't need a psychology degree to figure out that she'd identified with Scarlett O'Hara losing everything. He'd figured her latching on to an iconoclastic heroine was better than developing a drug addiction or identifying with some goth singer who looked like the Grim Reaper and wore makeup. His sister, however, was amazingly well-adjusted considering her childhood. "It's a wonder she hasn't tried to change the name of the place to Tara."

A spontaneous smile—as opposed to her usual I-have-to-be-nice-to-this-asshole smile—curved her lips and lit her eyes. "She did." It left Beau with the oddest feeling that he and Natalie shared a bond. "Cash put his foot down on that. He said they had to respect the history of the place."

He nodded. Much as he didn't want to, he felt a measure of grudging respect for Vickers on that. Beau knew from experience that telling Caitlyn *no* wasn't easy. He also gave Vickers points on standing behind Belle Terre's history.

"Beautiful Land is certainly a fitting name." The house sat on a knoll with gently rolling green hills beyond it. The Miscanauga Creek lay at the foot of the slope to the right rear of the house.

"It is, isn't it?" She pressed the button to release her seat belt. "Shall we start with the outside since we seem to be losing daylight?"

"Sure, sugar pie." That ought to grit her teeth and kill the camaraderie he felt squeezing in with the sexual tension that was thick enough to cut. Sexual tension he could deal with—revel in, in fact. Camaraderie was outside his realm of experience. "You've got something to take notes on?"

Her smile tightened around the edges but she kept it in place. She held up a notebook. "Right here, sugar pie." Touché. "Just let me know when you're ready." She tugged at her seat belt, a frown blooming between her delicately arched brows. "It's stuck."

He very seldom had passengers but he recalled that belt had wanted to stick the last time Scooter rode with him to the parts store. "Come to think of it, it's been kind of temperamental lately."

"Temperamental?"

"Yeah. You know, a little stubborn. Difficult. Let me see what I can do." He grinned. "It just needs the right touch."

"Oh, and you have it?" Something hot and sexual and exciting danced between them.

"It's worth a try since you're not doing such a hot job releasing yourself." His voice came out all warm and gravelly because he'd just painted a picture in his mind of her stretched out on his bed, her head thrown back, that mane of thick hair hanging over the side of his mattress as her fingers delved between her spread thighs, stroking, her brown eyes hot and sultry, her breath coming in short, quick pants as she sought gratification.

He reached across the expanse separating them

and his fingers encountered hers. She jerked her hand away, as if she felt the same rush he did. "There's a button…" he said, the backs of his fingers pressing against the curve of her hip. "You have to touch it just right—not too hard." She turned her head and her delectable mouth was right there. His jeans seemed to shrink, growing tighter across his crotch.

He pressed the button. Nothing happened. He pressed again. He shifted. "Got to find the sweet spot." The tip of her tongue peeked between her lips and left a moist glistening trail between the plump pinkness of her lips. Did she know she was slowly killing him? He was pretty sure she didn't. Still stuck. "C'mon, baby, let go," he coaxed.

The seat belt, if anything, pulled tighter against her chest, throwing her breasts into distracting relief.

"Can you, uh, see what you're doing?" She sounded breathless.

He was damn glad to hear it. Breathing was an increasing challenge on his end.

"I don't have to see. It's all in the touch."

"Well, obviously you don't have it any more than I do."

"Let me try from another angle." He got out and walked around to the passenger side. He opened the door and leaned in, across her. Her breath gusted warm against his neck even as her scent slipped around him. His arm brushed against her right breast as he leaned in. Totally an accident, but the result was the same. Her indrawn breath seemed to echo the tightening and clenching low in his belly.

He pressed the button and tugged, but it didn't budge. "I can't get it out."

A breeze blew through the open truck doors and a few strands of her hair danced along his jaw.

"Maybe you should try lubricating it."

"I've got just the thing." He stepped to the toolbox in the back and quickly returned. She was still sitting there strapped in. There was no way he could've deliberately jammed the seat belt but this was perfect. Well, kind of perfect because she didn't look nearly as pissed off as some women would've been. Actually, she didn't look pissed off at all as she tried to release the jammed mechanism.

Why hadn't he ever noticed before how sexy a woman could look with a seat belt bisecting her chest? He'd have to be a dead man to not see the way it showcased her breasts, tugging her shirt tight over them, her nipples outlined in taut ball-tightening relief. He wasn't anywhere close to dead.

"WD-40," he said.

He reached between her and the seat belt to spread a clean work rag over her thigh and hip. "Scooter's already got me paying for one outfit. I don't want to buy another. By the way, are you always getting into jams?"

She sputtered…actually sputtered, but her brown eyes sparkled with laughter and desire. "You… I… Ohhh."

"Hmm. Should I take that as a yes or a no?"

"You should take that as a *you* are a bad luck omen. I never had these kinds of problems before." But there was no real ire in her voice, and her eyes had darkened.

"You're debunking all kinds of myths for me. I expected a wedding planner to be more even-tempered."

"You seem to bring out the best in me."

"Ah, am I tapping into your inner bad girl?"

She shook her head, sending her thick fall of hair on that sinuous slide over her shoulders that he found so hot. "I don't have an inner bad girl."

He didn't believe it for a minute. "How disappointing." The flash of heat in her eyes told a different story. "I think you've got plenty of bad girl just waiting to be released."

"You are so wrong."

"Am I?" He abandoned the seat belt and reached up to wrap a thick curl around his finger. "Are you sure? There aren't any wicked bad-girl thoughts running through your head right now?"

"Maybe one…or two."

She parted her luscious lips and tilted her chin in a classic invitation to a kiss.

"Ah, Natalie has a naughty side…"

HEAVEN HELP HER but she wanted to kiss Beau Stillwell. Ever since she'd walked in and seen him nearly naked, she'd wanted this. It was as if he were some dark angel sent to torture her. And if she hadn't wanted him before, his gravel-filled "Naughty Natalie" did the trick.

Beau released her hair to trace the line of her jaw with one finger. He angled his head and her breath quickened in anticipation. She slid her hand around the back of his neck, her fingers testing his corded muscles.

He brushed his mouth over hers. Sampling. Coaxing. Teasing. Nice. She kissed him back. A civil exchange.

Totally unexpected, he swept his tongue against her lower lip and then dragged it into his mouth between his own lips—a delicious faint scrape of teeth and then a sucking.

"You have the most delectable, decadent mouth," he murmured and then proceeded to make delectable, decadent love to her mouth. She strained into him. Restricted by the seat belt, she pulled him closer.

They nipped, licked and then segued into hot, hungry, openmouthed kisses. She moaned in the back of her throat, a wordless entreaty. His big hands found her breasts, and nothing had ever felt as good as his mouth on hers and his hands cupping her through her clothing, his palms rubbing against her erect points. She arched her back, pushing her nipples harder into his hands. Hungry. So hungry.

He released her mouth and unleashed a tormenting torrent of kisses down her neck, his tongue dipping and delving along her collarbone. It wasn't enough. Not nearly enough. She tugged his head further down and then his mouth was on her breast, mouthing her through her cotton spandex T-shirt and her bra. He caught her tip in his teeth, and the light abrasion sent her into the stratosphere. Her eyes fluttered closed when he drew her into his wet mouth, suckling her through the cloth.

Where or when it would've ended she'd never know, because in the very dim recesses of her still-functioning mind, she registered the sound of an approaching vehicle.

She pushed against his shoulders, her breathing frantic gasps. "Someone's coming."

A little more time and it could've been her. What, what, what had she been thinking?

His blue eyes glittered when he raised his head and looked beyond her shoulder through the back window. He shook his head slightly, as if clearing it. "Tilson Dobbs. He's a retired Marine who's handling security for the place. I'll go check in with him." She was still trapped by the seat belt. He glanced down her chest to the wet, puckered material. "You might want to button your jacket."

5

HE MIGHT JUST HAVE TO kick Tilson's ass. They'd spent an hour and a half now going over the exterior and the downstairs, listing the necessary repairs and remodel required for the wedding and reception. Natalie actually had a good eye and an equally good grasp of what Caitlyn wanted done. But for the last hour and a friggin' half, Tilson had stuck to them like glue.

When Tilson had driven up, Beau had explained he was checking out the house and Tilson had been all set to ride his Mule, the all-terrain vehicle he drove over the property, off into the sunset to "secure the perimeter." And then Natalie had emerged from the cab of the truck. She'd resourcefully loosened the seat belt straps by pulling them and then climbed out.

Tilson had taken one look at her tousled hair and kiss-swollen lips and decided the perimeter didn't need securing nearly as much as he needed to check out the new female on the Dahlia horizon. Beau was pretty damn tired of Tilson trotting along with them and he didn't care for the way he kept eyeing Natalie. Sort of like a dog circling a juicy bone.

The guy was a persistent son of a bitch, Beau thought as Tilson followed them out of the house, into the now-dark night. They were finished making their list so Tilson could vamoose. Beau flicked on his flashlight and Natalie pulled out a pink one.

"Y'all want to grab some dinner now that you've wrapped things up out here?" Tilson asked as they covered the distance to the truck.

Beau cut him off at the pass. "We ate at Headlights on the way out here."

"How about grabbing a cup of coffee and a piece of pie at the Waffle House, then?" Tilson didn't even pretend to include Beau in that invite. "I can give you a ride to your car afterwards."

Once again, Beau didn't give Natalie a chance to answer. He opened the truck door for her, light from the dome spilling out into the dark, and said to Tilson, "We've got to discuss scheduling on the way back to her car. Got to use that time wisely."

Hell no, he wasn't feeling proprietary at the thought of Tilson nibbling at the fullness of her lower lip or mouthing her tightly budded nipple through her T-shirt the way he himself had earlier. Not a whit, because Beau didn't do proprietary with women. They were fun, a good time was had by all, and he moved on. Nope. It was simply that Natalie taking off with Tilson didn't fit in with his plan. That was all. Nothing more.

Natalie shot Beau a look that promised more to say

on the matter later. However, she said to Tilson as she slid into the cab, "Thanks, but we do need to wrap up the business."

Beau closed her door. "See ya, Tilson," he said as he rounded the truck to his side. Tilson looked decidedly unhappy but that wasn't Beau's problem, now was it?

Natalie sat buckled in the middle. She gestured to the mess next to her. "That seat belt is done for. I can't get the buckle loose and the belts won't retract."

He grinned and slid in next to her. "I'm not complaining." He buckled up and they headed back to the drag strip.

They weren't touching but he felt her body heat with mere inches separating her hips, thighs and shoulder from his. He caught an occasional whiff of her perfume, or maybe it was just her shampoo and the smell of her skin, but he liked it. He was more than ready to take up where they'd left off when Tilson had arrived.

"Just to set the record straight. I'm a big girl and fully capable of answering for myself."

What? Like he was just going to sit back while Tilson moved in and screwed up his plans? Not likely. Plus, she didn't have any business getting involved with the former Marine.

"Tilson's wife left him while he was on his last tour of duty in Iraq. He has issues." There. *Issues* was one of those girly buzzwords he heard his mother and sister and their friends use. He'd give her something to relate to and reveal his softer, feminine side.

"So, that's why you acted like such a jerk."

Obviously his softer, feminine side hadn't come through. "Don't you think *jerk's* a little harsh?"

"Harsh? I gave you the benefit of the doubt."

"I was being thoughtful. Gallant, even. I only had your best interest at heart."

She snorted. "And there I was thinking you were simply being manipulative and high-handed. Regardless, I'm fully capable of making my own decisions. And just for the record, Tilson's not my cup of tea."

He knew a moment of smug satisfaction. He nodded. "What is your type?"

"Suit and tie. Professional."

That was no real surprise. "Ah, a sissy boy with soft hands. Someone who doesn't break a sweat to do his job."

"I prefer to think of it as brains rather than brawn."

Maybe. And she could go on about brains and a suit and tie all day long, but he'd bet his racecar her panties had been wet earlier. "I'd say someone easily managed, who asks how high when you say jump. I think you have control issues."

She sputtered, actually, honest to God sputtered. "I…you…you…" And then she laughed, more with incredulity than amusement. "*You* think *I* have control issues? Okay."

He could tell there was so much more she wanted to say, except she was working for his sister. He bit back a chuckle. He'd like to hear what she *wasn't* saying.

"So, do you have one of those sissy boys on a string back in Nashville? I'm just asking because I'm not so sure he'd approve of the way you kissed me earlier."

"Wait a minute! You're seriously confused if you think I kissed you. You kissed me."

He hazarded a glance her way in the dashboard glow. Was that a flash of devilment in her brown eyes?

"No confusion here. And I can tell you now, sugar, if you were mine, I wouldn't want you kissing someone else that way."

He sensed—no, felt—the shift in her before she ever took action or opened her mouth. He'd pushed her to her limit. "Really? And if I were yours, be still my beating heart, how would you want me to kiss someone else?"

She released her seat belt. and before he could draw a breath she had twisted and curled one leg beneath her, levering herself up and bracing one hand on his shoulder, her warm breath teasing against his neck. "Like this?" She nuzzled beneath his ear and then nipped the tip of his lobe.

Holy hell. The sensation shot straight to his dick. She caught the recently nipped spot between her lips and sucked. His balls tightened as surely as if she'd cupped them in her hot little hands and gently squeezed.

He acknowledged the contest of wills. "No, baby, definitely not like that."

"Then what about this? Would this be acceptable?" She trailed hot, open mouthed kisses down the column of his neck and he was damn glad to see the drag strip entrance to his left because at this point he was DUI—driving under the influence of her distracting mouth.

He pulled into the spot next to her minivan in the nearly deserted lot and threw his truck into Park. "Definitely not acceptable."

He released his seat belt, turned and reached for her. She intercepted him, pushing him until his back was against the door, and leaned up on her knees. "Then maybe this?" Her mouth skated over his and she delivered light, flirty kisses that had his heart thumping out of control. Her hair tickled against his neck and he spanned her waist with his hands.

"Or this," she murmured against his mouth and then moved on to deep, soulful kisses. She captured his tongue and sucked and stroked it with hers. Stroke, suck, stroke, suck. It was a mind-numbing, cock-hardening, ball-tightening rhythm. If she could do that to his tongue he'd love to have her work that magic on his cock. He groaned into her mouth.

She pulled back and started to slide across the seat. "Did you find that acceptable?"

FIRE. She was playing with fire. She was *on* fire. While it was true that Beau had provoked her, she'd *wanted* to kiss him again. She needed to get out of here while she could still think about something other than how good he felt and tasted and the achy, hot need coiling tighter and tighter inside her.

Before she could move any further, he reached out, wrapped his big hands around her arms and hauled her back to the solid hardness of his body. "I'm still trying to decide if that's acceptable. I think I need a replay."

Her heart hammered against her ribs and a rush of wet heat surged between her thighs. If she had an ounce of sense, she'd skedaddle. He'd sort of man-handled her into his lap but she didn't feel threatened. If she insisted, he'd let her go. Deep inside, she knew he was one of the good guys. But apparently her last ounce of sense had abandoned her because she didn't want to leave. Instead, she wanted to flirt and tease and kiss him some more.

"You should pay closer attention the first time around," she said. She ended on a tiny gasp as he bent his head and nuzzled at her neck, and then she felt the faint scrape of his teeth followed by the velvet stroke of his tongue. That felt so *good.* She moaned and closed her eyes.

"Maybe I just wanted seconds…" he said in a husky murmur as he worked his way up her neck, "…or thirds."

She laughed softly and wound her arms around him. She'd only *thought* she was on fire before. His mouth found hers and she was drowning in the magic of his kiss. She molded the ridges of his muscular shoulders. He slid his hands beneath the edge of her T-shirt and spanned her waist. He stroked upward until his big hands cupped her breasts. She pushed harder against his fingers and he dipped them into her bra, finding the hardened tip. His fingers… his mouth…she pulled away and drew a ragged, gasping breath.

Severe tactical error on her part. She was about one kiss away from being in way over her head.

She tugged her shirt back down and slid across the seat to the passenger side. He let her go, but there was no mistaking the glint in his eyes.

"If you were mine," he said, "I'd have to vote for you not kissing anyone else at all, in any way at all."

She snatched up her purse and opened the passenger door. "Then I guess it's a good thing I'm not yours."

She slammed the door behind her.

MONDAY MORNING, Natalie looked up from her day planner on her Queen Anne desk in the back corner of the bridal shop as the bell jangled over the front door.

"It's just me," Cynthia called out.

Natalie was doubly glad to see her assistant. Not only did she genuinely like Cynthia, she was more than ready for a distraction. She desperately needed to think about something, someone other than Beau Stillwell. Living above her shop was convenient on several fronts. She didn't have a commute. She saved on rent.

The downside was she'd never really had a space all her own. Growing up, from as early as she could remember, she'd shared her room, and clothes and toys with foster siblings. And now she shared her home space with her business. One day, she wanted a house of her own. But, for now, she'd take advantage of no commute and always being in the office, ready for the day, by seven-thirty. This morning, however, Natalie had hit the office at six-thirty, ready to lose herself in work, details, planning—anything but thinking about Beau.

Although she was tired last night, nothing had satisfied her. She'd run a bubble bath when she got home, dumping a generous portion of lavender bath salts in. Between the warm water and aromatherapy she should've been out like a light. Nope. She'd tried reading a book. Not interested. Nothing on television. She'd popped in *Pride and Prejudice*—A&E's Colin Firth as Mr. Darcy, thank you very much—but not even *P&P* struck a chord for her.

She'd finally admitted to herself that she was sexually keyed up and taken matters into her own hands. It was a rather sad fact, but the truth of the matter was that not all orgasms were created equal. She'd had her orgasm but she'd still felt all empty and achy and needy inside.

Masturbation simply didn't mimic the nuzzle of Beau's mouth on her neck or the delicious pressure of his hand and mouth on her breast. And the very thought of his mouth between her wet thighs... Yeah, that had been the fantasy that sent her right on over the edge to hollow satisfaction. Kissing him had been analogous to playing with fire. She hadn't gotten burned, but she was definitely singed. How could a man so wrong, so different from what she wanted in a man, turn her on so thoroughly, so completely?

And it didn't matter. This, too, would pass. She'd finally gotten him out to Belle Terre. Now all she needed was the schedule from him, which she could most likely go through his secretary for, and she was done with Beau Stillwell until she had to see him again at the rehearsal dinner. Months. Woohoo.

"How was your Sunday?" Natalie asked as Cynthia put away her purse and beelined for the hot water in the back. Natalie wandered into the stockroom behind her and leaned against the doorjamb.

"I spent most of the day parked on the sofa reading a romance novel, just to remind myself there are decent men out there, and eating popcorn. But I didn't cry. Not even once." Cynthia measured out loose English breakfast tea leaves into the stainless steel ball.

Natalie would've hugged her, except Cynthia wasn't the hugging type. The last couple of months had been tough for her assistant. Cynthia had been expecting a proposal from her live-in boyfriend, Josh, after two years together. Instead, she'd gotten the news that Josh was going to be a daddy—the sticking point being that Cynthia wasn't the mommy. And he'd even robbed her of the pleasure of kicking him to the curb. He'd moved out and sent her a text message breaking both pieces of news while Natalie and Cynthia had been in the middle of directing a rehearsal. Bastard.

"Good," Natalie said. "That's real progress. Double good because he's so not worth it."

Tears shimmered in Cynthia's eyes but she squared her shoulders and raised her chin. "But enough about me. Did you get the remodel schedule down? What was the race like?" She cocked her head to one side and assessed Natalie, her lips pursed. "And what's different about you this morning? You definitely look different."

"We got the remodel list made. We didn't get as far as the schedule. The race was, believe it or not, kind of exciting. And I suppose this is what I look like when I'm losing my mind."

Cynthia dropped the tea ball into the hot water. "Why do I get the feeling we're not talking about your standard garden-variety lose-your-mind?"

Natalie brought her up to speed on most of the day while Cynthia opened a Pop-Tart and dropped it into the toaster. "His pieces aren't quite fitting together. His crew member tells me the guy can remember stats from two races ago but I have to schlep along behind him like a hired hand, taking notes. That doesn't add up."

"So what are you saying?"

"I don't know. See, that's the problem. I can't think

straight." There. She'd admitted it. He was messing with her head.

"So, call Shelby up and grill her about this guy. That girl loves to talk."

It was true. Her younger foster sister was a motor-mouth, which was great considering the quiet, with-drawn kid she'd been when she'd shown up as a thirteen-year old. Natalie was adaptable and she got along well with almost all the kids her parents took in, but she and Shelby had really bonded. "She's never met him."

"It doesn't matter," Cynthia said, stirring a spoon-ful of sugar into her tea. "There's no way Caitlyn didn't talk about her home life, about him. Find out what Shelby knows."

Shelby had had plenty to say about how overpro-tective Caitlyn's big brother could be, but that was simply from overhearing conversations and Caitlyn's complaints.

"I don't want her to think I'm…" Natalie hesitated.

"You're what?"

Natalie crossed her arms over her chest. "You know…interested." She gave a one-shoulder shrug. "Personally or anything."

Cynthia's spoon clanged against the side of the cup and her mouth dropped open. "Oh my God, you are, aren't you?"

"Definitely not. So not my type. And he's obnoxious. And he wastes my time. And I made out with him." She buried her face in her hand.

"Sheep shit on a stick. You made out with him? Define '*made out*.'"

"You know, he kissed me. Then later I kissed him." She left out the part about masturbating to the thought of him going down on her. Some things were just better left unsaid.

"I'm totally confused. I thought you said he's obnoxious."

"He is."

They left the stockroom.

"And you were kissing him, why?"

"To prove a point…and he is obnoxious…in a hot way. I mean, not hot according to my standards but hot according to a lot of other standards." Natalie dropped back into the chair at her desk and Cynthia perched on one of the two chairs on the other side.

"Right. That just clears everything up…not. Exactly what point were you proving by making out with him?"

It had made sense at the time. "It's complicated."

"Apparently. I can't wait to meet him. He's the first man I've ever seen get you all discombobulated."

"I am not discombobulated. Okay, well, maybe a little." And she didn't want to think about him anymore. She'd already thought about him half the night. Make that three-quarters of the night. She was now desperately trying to adhere to out of sight, out of mind before she got to just plain old out of her mind. "Sara Gastoneau is coming in this morning—"

Natalie's cell phone interrupted with the instantly recognizable Mendelssohn's "Wedding March" from *A Midsummer Night's Dream.* Her clients loved that ring tone and so did she. The traditional recessional signaled yet another wedding completed and the start of a new life together as husband and wife. Caller ID flashed Caitlyn Stillwell's name.

"Natalie! You are such a doll."

"Hi, Caitlyn," Natalie said with a smile. Caitlyn Stillwell possessed an infectious enthusiasm. "How's life on the road and why am I a doll?"

Caitlyn offered a dreamy sigh at the other end. "Life on the road is wonderful…mostly because I'm with Cash. But we're getting some great video footage." That had been a biggie among many challenges in planning their wedding. Not only was it on short notice, but the bride-to-be was touring the country by bus with her fiancé and shooting video footage for what they hoped would be a reality show or documentary. Natalie had never planned a wedding before with the bride out of town. "And you're a doll because I just got off of the phone with Beau. You are the best."

Why did that have an ominous ring? "I'm glad you think so but I'm not sure I'm following you here."

"He told me about you helping him out at Belle Terre."

"No problem." Sometimes her business called for a little white lie. "I was more than happy to help." He'd wasted several hours of her time. And sometimes it was a whopping white lie.

"I bet no other wedding planner would do what you're doing. Even Cash is impressed."

Yay! This was exactly the response she wanted, exactly what she wanted Caitlyn to put out to the public. Once Caitlyn and Cash were married, Caitlyn would be Nashville royalty.

"That's why I'm here. I don't want you stressing about the wedding. I just want you to have fun and look forward to it."

Caitlyn laughed on the other end. "I'll admit I was stressing a little over the renovations, but now that you're personally assisting Beau with the remodel and building…"

What the hell? She wasn't personally assisting him with anything now that they'd made that list. "He swears he'd never be able to get the project done in time for the wedding if you weren't willing to come out and help him with the project," Caitlyn steamed on. "Cash and I think you're the best."

She'd already said that once. Natalie forced a smile into her voice, "Well, I'm not sure how much—"

Caitlyn interrupted. "Don't be modest. Beau said not many professionals would be willing to go that extra mile of meeting him at Belle Terre at six-thirty in the morning and then again in the evenings to work around your other projects. He was impressed with your flexibility."

"Coming from him that means a lot." She couldn't help her dark sarcasm. And it was better than screaming. What was he up to? Because he was definitely up to something. They'd no more discussed her squeezing renovation help into her already packed schedule than she had monkeys flying out her tush. Hel-lo. It was high wedding season. She was *busy*. But she couldn't say that to Caitlyn. He'd pretty much manipulated Natalie into a tight spot.

"Hey, can you hold on a minute, Natalie?" On the other end, someone was talking to Caitlyn. "Yeah… Okay… Right… I'm just wrapping up here. Hey, I'm back but I've gotta go. Call me if anything else comes up. Otherwise, I'll talk to you later."

The phone clicked in Natalie's ear. She turned to Cynthia, who'd eavesdropped unabashedly. Not that she blamed her for that.

"I guess it would be counterproductive," Natalie said, "to kill him *before* the renovation is done and he's walked her down the aisle, huh?"

It was sheer annoyance at his blatant manipulation that had Natalie's heart pounding and not the thought of being in close proximity to his wickedly distracting mouth and hands and his big, hard body.

No, *that* particular thought was responsible for her now-damp panties.

6

BEAU WHISTLED UNDER his breath as he made his way back to his truck, satisfied his roofing crew was set on the new subdivision job he'd contracted between Nashville and Dahlia. Urban sprawl was both a bane and a blessing, but right now it was a damn fine morning in Dahlia. The sun was shining, he had jobs lined up in a less-than-stellar economy and he had Natalie Bridges right where he wanted her.

He leaned against the cab of his truck and checked his wristwatch. He'd finished up the conversation with his sister about forty-five minutes ago. He figured he'd get a call anytime now. Actually, depending on how long Caitlyn kept Natalie on the phone, it could be another couple of minutes.

Natalie. Her sweet, hot mouth…her velvet tongue… Classy. Sexy. Fiery. True enough, he'd started out with the intent to shut this wedding down and that remained his primary goal, but he'd discovered two things in the last day. One, he realized he'd never had to chase a woman before. From the earliest time he could remember women just seemed to like him. But

Natalie brought out the hunter in him. Two, he wanted her. She'd told him yesterday in no uncertain terms he wasn't her type. Bullshit. She wouldn't… couldn't…kiss him that way if she didn't want him.

He scrolled through his cell-phone options. Natalie deserved her own ringtone and he deserved to be forewarned when she called. He downloaded and waited.

He didn't have to wait long. His phone trilled the opening chords of AC/DC's "Highway to Hell."

"I just spoke to Caitlyn," she said without preamble.

A fly buzzed past him and the sounds of the guys hauling up shingle bundles and recounting weekend exploits filled the background. "Great. I'm sure it's important to stay in close contact when you're planning her wedding."

He climbed in the cab of the truck, cutting off the background noise. He could've sworn on the drive from his office to the work site that he'd caught the occasional whiff of her scent from last night.

"You know, press-ganged servitude is out of vogue these days. Of course, I have only myself to blame." She paused and sighed heavily on the other end. "I should've never kissed you."

What angle was she working? Women never regretted kissing him. Quite the opposite, in fact.

"I'll have to say you've lost me there, sweet thing." He picked up the take-out coffee cup from the dash cup holder. Empty.

"Obviously I drove you beyond the point of desperate when I kissed you," she announced on a smug note. "It goes without saying I'd never go out with you, so you've resorted to manipulating me into indentured servitude."

She'd never go out with him, as if he were some substandard species? The hell, she said. The hunt was definitely on. He chuckled.

"Indentured servitude?" Well, hell, that just brought a whole bunch of things to mind. Her on her knees in front of him, her mouth on his…a little light bondage with silken cords… "Does that mean you want me to tie you up?"

"You wouldn't dare." Well, well, well. She sounded far more breathless than outraged. Just what was going on in her pretty little head? "And can you say sexual harassment?"

No. And neither could she. "Am I writing your paycheck, baby? Do I have the authority to fire or promote you? Think again. If you find yourself all tied up, it's strictly because that's what you want."

"I think you have a pretty accurate idea of what I want right now and it's not that." No man with a brain would trust that sweet note.

"I'm certain I know *what* you want, you just need to decide *how* you want it."

"Since you seem to be calling all the shots at this point, you tell me. When do you want to start?"

"I'm sitting on ready. You're the one with the rushed time schedule. Let's start this evening."

"What time?"

"Six." That ought to have her sitting through Nashville rush hour. The idea, after all, was to push her to her limits.

"Perfect."

Perfect? Ha. She was probably ready to gnaw on wood. And just to thoroughly piss her off… "And don't be late. I'd hate for us to get behind schedule because you're not punctual."

He could all but feel her kiss-my-ass radiating over the phone line. Perversely, he was looking forward to 6:00 p.m.

AT PRECISELY four-thirty, Natalie pulled into a parking spot on Dahlia's picturesque town square. There was no way she was going to sit through rush-hour traffic heading out of the city. Plus, she'd seen Beau's face when Scooter told her to replace her outfit at Stillwell Motors Racing's expense. Two could play his game, and she was more than willing to hit below the belt…at least, that's where she assumed he kept his wallet.

She slung her purse over her shoulder and locked the minivan. Was it her imagination or did the air smell sweeter, fresher here? With its refurbished store fronts around a parklike square anchored by a Confederate soldier monument, Dahlia was a refreshing step back in time—especially after the urban sprawl that had become Nashville.

She'd driven through with Caitlyn once before on their way out to Belle Terre and Caitlyn had pointed out the green and white striped awning that marked Beverly's Closet, but they hadn't stopped. Now Natalie strolled along the sidewalk, enchanted.

Early on, she and Caitlyn had discussed whether to use local businesses in the wedding or Natalie's tried-and-true Nashville contacts. Now that Caitlyn had made up her mind, Natalie needed to set up appointments to meet with the business owners. True, she could just drop in, but that seemed disrespectful of their time— and thank you, Beau Stillwell, she knew all about how it felt to have someone disregard your time.

Plus, she wouldn't mind an opportunity to "window-shop" anonymously. One of her concerns was whether the small hometown businesses in Dahlia could deliver and pull off an event like Caitlyn and Cash's wedding. Not that she didn't want every wedding to be perfect, but the way this one would be covered by the media, Natalie's already narrow margin of error had narrowed even further. This, the career catalyst that had been handed to her like a gift, had to be as close to perfect as possible.

She'd noted the bakery's location on the outskirts of town, a pink cinder block building with white lace curtains gracing the display windows of Pammy's Petals. She paused now in front of Christa's Florals and breathed a small sigh of relief. Several elegant floral arrangements on a velvet runner filled the front window. Whew! It was always a bad sign when a florist presented funeral wreaths and cemetery flowers as their primary offering.

She passed a small gallery showing several stained-glass pieces, lace and beadwork and a lovely wedding-knot quilt in shades of lavender, yellow and pink that sent a wave of nostalgia washing over her. She could almost smell the signature scent of gardenia her grandmother had favored and feel her warmth as they'd shared a similar quilt on Memaw's front porch swing when Natalie had been a young girl. She blinked. It would be beyond crazy to burst into tears on the Dahlia sidewalk because some exquisitely crafted artwork had pulled an emotional rug out from under her feet.

She walked on. Dahlia Hair and Nails. Hmm. Hard to tell, but selling Caitlyn on another stylist would be a real challenge. Apparently the owner, Lila, was Caitlyn's mother's best friend.

She paused on the sidewalk outside Beverly's Closet, ostensibly admiring the ivy topiaries and spring-mix flowers in oversized planters flanking the glass door. She realized she was nervous. As the mother of the bride, Beverly had been part of the preplanning with Natalie and Caitlyn, and Natalie liked the older woman, but she was suddenly self-consciously aware that Beverly was also the mother of Natalie's new object of full-blown lust.

And like it or not, Beau hadn't just slipped into that spot, he'd commandeered it. Dear god, even when he was being manipulative and arrogant and every other unpleasant adjective she could throw his way, damn him to hell, he tripped her trigger.

And that was highly, impossibly problematic. He was everything she didn't want in a man, wasn't he? Relationships weren't supposed to shake you up and make you feel unsettled and as if you were too much for your own skin. And that was an equally crazy thought. What she and Beau had wasn't even close to a relationship. It was a…she didn't even know what it was. Wanting to strip a man naked and work her way up, or down, his body didn't qualify as a relationship.

As if that wasn't the craziest thing. She shrugged away the silly thought and stepped into Beverly's Closet.

At the tinkle of the bell, Beverly looked up from where she was plumping a cushion in an armchair upholstered in apple-green velvet. "Can I help you…" Recognition kicked in. "Natalie, it's so good to see you again. Come on in, sugar." Beverly's genuine smile encompassed her. Somewhere in her midfifties, with porcelain skin, moss-green eyes and shoulder-length hair dyed a soft, flattering shade of blond, Caitlyn's mother struck Natalie as the quintessential middle-aged Southern beauty.

Beverly hugged her, engulfing her in a cloud of perfume. "What a nice surprise. Well, not a total surprise because Milton called and explained the ruined outfit." A delicate blush tinged Beverly's porcelain cheeks.

"Milton?" Natalie didn't know anyone named Milton.

"Milton Lewis."

Lewis? That sounded familiar but it wouldn't click into place. And obviously she still looked perplexed.

"Beau's crew chief."

Right. "Oh. *That* Mr. Lewis." Natalie laughed. She'd really liked Scooter, née Milton, Lewis. "I didn't think his mother named him Scooter."

Beverly rolled her eyes in exasperation. "Isn't that the most ridiculous thing you ever heard to call a grown man? He picked up that name in high school when he and my late husband started tinkering with cars. Since Milton was the shortest, he'd scoot underneath the car to work on it."

Natalie personally preferred Scooter to Milton, but she kept her own counsel. She'd quickly learned in this business when to hold her tongue. Well, most of the time. When she was around Beau, however, she didn't manage nearly as well. "Hmm." She, however, found Beverly's blush sweet. "So, Mr. Lewis called you?"

Color rose in the older woman's cheeks again. "To tell me you might come by."

"Uh-huh," Natalie responded with a knowing smile. Beverly was a beautiful woman and, well, bottom line, Scooter or Milton or whatever they called him was a man.

Another delicate stain of pink blossomed. "We talked for a while. I think he's lonely since Emma Jean died."

"And I think you're a beautiful woman."

"Well…why…thank you. That's what he said, too," Beverly told her in a sudden rush. She buried her hands in her face momentarily and then looked up, equal measures of excitement and mortification in her green eyes. "Oh, Lord, he asked me to go to dinner."

Natalie had the distinct impression she'd just wandered into something intensely personal but was enough of a stranger to qualify as a confidante. And for whatever reason, people seemed to confide in her. "What did you say?"

"I said I'd let him know."

Absence of a flat-out *no* meant *yes*. "Do you want to go?"

Beverly fluttered her hand nervously along her hairline. "I don't know…it's been so long… What if he tries to kiss me when he brings me home?"

Natalie pushed aside the memory of Beau's mouth on her lips and breast that seemed seared into her brain. This wasn't about her and this woman's son. Regardless, her entire body went on red alert and her nipples stood at attention. She was pretty damn sure she was wearing her own blush now. "Do you want him to?"

Straightening a row of hangers that didn't need straightening, Beverly avoided eye contact. "It's not that. I haven't... It's been... Monroe, Beau and Caitlyn's daddy, died sixteen years ago and I haven't *seen*—" she glanced up meaningfully "—anyone since then."

Seen? Natalie's curiosity and confusion must have shone in her face.

"My children needed me and I was all torn up inside, and then when Caitlyn was older, I thought it was still best not to date and it's just gotten to be a habit. What if I don't remember how to kiss? And what will my children think? What would you think if *your* mother was about to start dating?"

She'd never thought about it. She took a second to consider, unwilling to throw out a glib response to something that was obviously so important to Beverly. "I think if my dad died I wouldn't want my mother to be lonely. I think your kids will feel the same. Maybe not at first...but they'll come around. Well, I think Caitlyn's so wrapped up in the engagement and wedding and love in general that she'll be right onboard."

Beverly nodded. "I think you're right. I'm more worried about Beau. He stepped right in as man of the family when Monroe passed." The tension in the set of Beverly's shoulders eased. Apparently she was more comfortable discussing her son and the past, even if it was a difficult time, than a future date and potential kiss with Scooter. "Lord, he was only sixteen but he finished school and worked in the evenings and on the weekends and we made ends meet. I cleaned houses to keep our heads above water but Beau's the reason I have this business and the house I'm in now." There was no denying the admiration and mother's pride shining in her eyes. "That boy has worked his tail off to provide a home and this business for me and he's made sure Caitlyn never wanted for anything she truly needed. He became a man at sixteen."

Something warm and dangerous flip-flopped inside Natalie. In retrospect, she supposed she'd heard bits and pieces of this story from her sister, Shelby, but had not really paid much attention. She didn't want to think of Beau as a man who mentored Tim, his now-fatherless pit-crew member, or busted his young butt to keep a roof over his mother's and sister's heads. That all ran counter to dismissing him as just another hot, albeit arrogant, guy. She realized, rather lamely, that a somewhat expectant silence had stretched between them.

"I can see why you're proud of him. Hopefully he'll be okay with you going out with Scoot— I mean, Milton."

Beverly beamed, as if a tremendous weight had been lifted from her shoulders. "He'll just have to be, won't he?"

"And don't worry that you won't remember how to kiss. It's probably been a while for him, as well. Y'all can remember together."

Another blush, but somehow this looked more like a blush of expectation than embarrassment. She nodded, her eyes sparkling. "So, we need to outfit you because that son of mine was hard to track down." She clicked her tongue against the roof of her mouth. "I know he's busy but I taught him better manners than that. Exactly what got ruined?"

"Just a blouse and a jacket. That should cover it."

"Did the jacket go with a suit?" Beverly quirked a salon-arched brow.

"Well, yes."

She shook her head, clearly annoyed with the son she'd just venerated. "He knows better." Her eyes gleamed as she nodded. "An entire suit and blouse. I raised him better than that."

Natalie almost felt sorry for Beau Stillwell. And then she thought about him dragging her out to Belle Terre as if she didn't have anything better to do than his bidding on a construction project and offered Beverly her brightest smile.

7

NATALIE PULLED INTO the circular drive fronting Belle Terre and parked her minivan next to Beau's truck. She drew a deep, steadying breath. She was being ridiculous. It was just his lousy truck—granted, she'd had a heck of a good time in that front seat as recently as last night—and her heart was galloping in her chest. She couldn't seem to stop herself from a quick glimpse in the rearview mirror to check hair and makeup. No mascara smears, no oily spots on her face—blotting papers were a beautiful thing—and her lip gloss was fine. She smoothed down a spot where her hair was sticking up. Good to go.

She climbed out of the car and approached the house. It was imposing and, if she was totally honest, a little scary. While beautiful, there was an air of melancholy about it, but then again, how many generations had loved, lived, cried and died here? How could a place that had once held people in captivity as slaves to a master know anything but melancholy, despite the laughter that must have spilled from the shuttered windows that opened to the soaring, columned porch?

Beau opened the front door—apparently waiting on her to show up, she noted—and all philosophical and esoteric thought fled in light of her purely physical response to six foot plus of dark-haired, blue-eyed, well-muscled man in jeans, T-shirt and work boots. What had happened to her penchant for suits and ties? Gone. System bypassed in favor of hot and rugged standing with splayed legs in the doorway. Sweet, hot, immediate desire flooded her.

"You're here," he said, his dark-lashed eyes sweeping her, touching her in a way that left her breathless.

She marched past him into the foyer. "I am." She strove to bring some semblance of detachment to the situation. She turned to face him, opting for the direct approach. "Now why don't you tell me why I'm really here? You could have a high-school kid help you and they'd be more adept at this than me."

Those eyes flickered over her again and it was a replay of the scene in *The Libertine* when just one look from Johnny Depp and she was ready to crawl naked across the floor for him. "But you're the one with the insight into what Caitlyn wants done," he went on. "And after you—how was it exactly—oh, right, drove me beyond the point of desperate with those kisses…you really didn't leave me any choice, did you?"

She knew the moment that came out of her mouth she'd regret saying it. And she could only blame her lack of self-control on him. He was the culprit. There was something about him. He got under her skin. Wanting to crawl naked across a floor for him was a perfect case in point. She was good with crawling naked across the floor but not for *him*. She scrambled for some measure of sanity.

"I shouldn't have said that. Occasionally, my mouth runs away with me. And about the other, I've been thinking—"

He interrupted. "The other?"

She was altogether too, too aware that it was her and him alone in an empty house and to stand about throwing the word *kiss* or *kissing* around seemed dangerous territory. Couldn't they address the issue in a nice civilized roundabout manner? "You know what I mean."

He closed the front door with a final, resounding click. He approached her with a measured, intent tread, and her pulse hammered. "You've got to speak clearly and slowly for us he-man types who are more brawn than brains, sugar." He held out broad, masculine hands, palms up, as if for her inspection, approval. "These hands have calluses."

In less than a second, she was imagining the erotic scrape of those calluses against her sensitive nipples, down her body, between her legs. Pathetically, that sent a shiver through her and a rush of liquid warmth between her thighs.

"Kissing." Brief and to the point, and still the mere mention with him right in front of her left her tingling and aroused because her mind had taken her far, far beyond a mere merging of lips and tongues.

"Oh. That other." He grinned, an evil, wicked, I'd-like-to-seduce-you-right-out-of-your-panties grin that set her heart knocking against her ribs. He dropped his gaze to her mouth. "I'm all for it."

Good lord, she'd like to back him up against that door and eat him alive—especially when he looked at her like that. She grasped at the last few threads of sanity, reminding herself she was here to move this wedding forward and not to make out with Caitlyn's big sexy brother. "Well, I'm not."

His slow smile slid devastatingly up and down her spine. "Now you're making me feel inadequate as a man." Uh-huh. And there really was a Santa Claus. "I could've sworn you liked it."

If ever a man needed taking down a peg or two, she was looking at his wicked sexy self. "It was…" She tilted her head to one side and pretended to search for a description. She deliberately brightened, as if suddenly enlightened. "Adequate." She was dancing close to the flames again but she couldn't seem to help it.

"Oh, hell no." He shook his head. "I have standards and adequate isn't one of them." He took a step toward her and his slow, sexy smile spread a sweet heat of anticipation through her. "We're gonna have to work on this until we've passed adequate."

No, no and no. Kissing him had been like setting

a blowtorch to a marshmallow inside her. She'd never been one to hop in bed with a guy, but Beau seemed to knock every aspect of her off course. She had a sinking feeling that a little more kissing, she'd be hard-pressed to keep her legs together and her panties on. And that was an understatement. She was about two seconds from she wasn't exactly sure what, but it was dangerous.

She stepped back.

"You'll have to practice with someone else. I'm sure you won't have any problem locating a partner—" or two or ten, she thought, recalling the two women who'd stopped by post-race "—but it's not me. No more kissing."

He frowned in mock consternation, a wicked gleam in his bedroom-blue eyes. "Now that puts me in a downright awkward position, baby girl."

God, she was certifiably losing her mind because she found his *baby girl* incredibly sexy. "How is that awkward? Awkward is carrying on when we're supposed to be working."

He reached out and tilted her chin up with his fingertip. One touch—just his fingertip against her skin rendered her breathless. "I suppose I need clarification… Surprised you with that fancy word, didn't I? Do I go with this or do I kiss you when you ask me to?"

She pushed his hand away. "That's easy to answer… because I won't be asking."

"Right. You do like to take matters into your own hands." For one moment she was mortified that he knew he'd inspired her to fire up her vibrator last night. Then she realized he was referring to her showing up at the racetrack on Friday evening. "Then, for clarity's sake, just so I don't get into trouble—*when* you kiss me again, is it okay to kiss you back?"

She didn't miss his *when* rather than *if.* She crossed her arms over her chest. "Let me spell it out for you. No kissing. None. You're not kissing me. I'm not kissing you. I'm not asking. I'm not doing. Nada." Good. She'd sounded resolute. Strong. No hint there that she desperately wanted to taste him, touch him, and likewise feel his hands and his mouth on various and sundry parts of her.

Another one of those looks that tightened every cell in her body into acute, aching awareness that she was a woman. "That's too bad. Just kissed is a good look on you."

"I'll keep that in mind." Breathe. She needed to remember to breathe…and not kiss him…or take her clothes off. Work. Renovation. The matter at hand. "Now, to borrow one of your phrases, we're burning daylight. What do you need for me to do?"

"Since you just told me it's off-limits—" his glance zeroed in and lingered on her mouth, and the wanton fire inside her flamed a little hotter, higher, brighter "—I guess we'll skip to the second item on the list." A tsunami of turn-on assaulted her. One look. One moment of innuendo and she was wet, her nipples were hard and her clit ached.

"I need you to get on your knees..." He paused deliberately, and it was a small wonder she didn't spontaneously combust at the implication of her on her knees, his fly undone, his dick in her mouth. At this point he could probably talk her through an orgasm... which had never happened before but seemed totally one hundred percent plausible right here and now.

"...to scrape paint off the baseboards."

So much for her orgasm.

HE WAS HOISTED on his own petard, as his Grandpa Stillwell had been fond of saying. Beau had deliberately saddled Natalie with the most menial, uncomfortable task at hand. However, he hadn't counted on the effect of her on her knees, bending over, her tight, round ass thrust in the air.

"You know, if you make your stroke a little longer and smoother, it'll be better for you. Slow it down a little, baby girl, or you're going to wear yourself out before you even get started."

She looked back over her shoulder at him and he'd asked for it, he'd taken it there, but it was such a sexual look it slammed him in the gut.

Her cell phone went off in her purse, shattering the moment. She scrambled to get up off the floor, and he automatically scooped up her purse and handed it to her.

"Thanks," she said, her fingers glancing against his ever so briefly, but still rousing.

"You're welcome." Dammit to hell, every time they touched it was as if someone had yanked a rug out from under his feet.

She pulled out the phone and answered. "Hi, Mom... No, it's fine... I'm just working... I know... Right... Maybe sometime next week... No, I don't want Miguel to think I don't love him... No, I know it's important that he knows he's important to me."

Who in the hell was Miguel? And why'd her mother have to remind her that he needed to know he was important and that she loved him? He'd assumed, based on their conversation and the way she'd kissed him, there was no boyfriend in the picture.

"I'm just busy," she said.

Ignoring Beau, Natalie knelt down again and started scraping, propping the phone between her ear and her shoulder. Beau heard her mother's voice faintly over the line. He couldn't hear her words but he picked up on the gently remonstrative tone. He had no difficulty in discerning a Southern mama guilt trip, having been on the receiving end several times, most of the time for good reason.

"Look, Mom, I hate to cut this short but I see my appointment parking their car up front and I don't want to be on the phone when they walk in." The next part came out in a rush. "I'll see you next week. Love you."

She ended the call and shot Beau a look where he

stood propped against the staircase. "Don't say anything," she dared. "I know it was a lie, but you don't know my mother. Once she starts…"

Beau grinned. "You've met my mother? I totally understand." For a moment they both shared a laugh, her expression unguarded. The laughter died and he found himself looking into her motor oil-brown eyes and wanting…more. More than a kiss, more than her naked beneath him—although that would be damn nice. He had a hankering to *know* Natalie Bridges. What did she do when she wasn't busy aiding and abetting the attachment of ball and chain? And who the hell was Miguel?

"Who's Miguel?"

She went back to scraping, following his directive with a slow, smooth rhythm that put him in mind of her hand on his… Hell, who was he kidding? Her simply breathing seemed to put him in mind of her hand—or some equally stimulating body part—on his cock.

"My newest 'brother.' My parents foster kids. Miguel arrived last week and I haven't gotten out to meet him yet. I know. My parents are great, but they're…different."

Yeah, he'd be in much better shape to think about her parents than the slide of her smooth, soft hand against his hard… "Where do they live?"

"West of Nashville. They've got a farm with a big garden, chickens, ponies, a rambling farm house, and it's just crazy there." She shook her head, a sweet smile lifting the corners of her delicious mouth. "Always crazy. I can't tell you how many times I'd go to bed at night only to wake up and find a new sister in my room the next morning."

"It sounds—"

She rocked back on her heels, scraper in hand. "Chaotic. Total chaos. I lived for the times I could go to my grandparents' house. Memaw and I would sit on the porch swing at night and she'd tell me stories." She radiated a sweetly vulnerable nostalgia that tugged at him. He had an instant image of her as a pigtailed little girl curled up beside her grandmother. "The other kids would go over in twos or threes, but Memaw always insisted that when it was my turn, I was the only one allowed over. She knew I needed that alone time. And it made me feel special."

He nodded, sharing an understanding from his own childhood. "Nana, my dad's mother, and my mother got along about like oil and water, but Nana always made banana pudding when I came over. It's my favorite. She'd make a separate dish just for me and add extra bananas and vanilla wafers to it." He hadn't thought about Nana's pudding in years. He shook his head. "So is Shelby your biological sister or your foster sister?"

She set about scraping again, her hair falling forward in a wavy curtain of brown and red. "Foster."

She pushed her hair aside and slanted a glance his way. "And the answer to the next question that inevitably comes is, I don't have any biological siblings but I have twenty, well, twenty-one now with Miguel, siblings. And, no, they didn't all live there at once. The house is usually at full capacity with ten. But most of us come back for holidays and special occasions." She looked back down. "And they are all great, and I do feel guilty that I haven't met Miguel yet. You can't imagine Thanksgiving and Christmas. You'd have to see it to believe it." Both tenderness and exasperation marked her tone.

Paint flecks peppered her hair. "Are you trying to take me home to meet your mother already?"

Teasing her was too much fun. He couldn't pass up the opportunity.

She made a noise that sounded suspiciously like a snort. "My mother would like you." Beau preened. "She likes anyone and everyone…regardless of how annoying they are."

Beau guffawed, his laughter coming from deep in his belly. "Smart-ass."

She grinned and he felt the same knock-you-on-your-ass sensation he did when he kicked it off the starting line in a race. "I was just saying…"

He wanted her with an intensity that was foreign to him, given he was always the one in control. The mood between them shifted, intensified, thickened. Her eyes widened.

Beau moved toward her, slowly, deliberately. "Do you always mean what you say?"

Had she really meant no more kissing? They both knew what he was asking.

She steadied herself with one hand on the floor and ran the tip of her tongue along the bow of her upper lip. There was no mistaking the flicker of heat in her eyes. "Not…always."

Green light. He reached down and dragged her up his body and into his arms. Her scent, the feel of her soft curves against his hard angles, the almost imperceptible hitch of her breath… Yes, he'd wanted this all last night, all day today. "Speak now, baby girl, or forever hold your peace if you meant what you said earlier."

The scraper clattered to the floor and she placed her open palms against his chest, tilting her head back to gaze up at him. "What if Tilson shows up? He did last night."

He slid his hand up her arm to trace the fine line of her jaw. Her skin felt like velvet against his fingertips. "Tilson won't show up. Trust me."

Her eyes darkened and her fingers curled against his chest, sending his inner temperature spiking off the charts. "How do you know?"

The fall of her hair teased against the back of his hand. "Tilson won't show up because I told him you were off-limits."

She went rigid. "You what?"

"Off-limits. I told him you were mine." He plied his thumb along the fullness of her lower lip and pulled her closer still with his other arm. "Natalie, baby girl, consider my claim staked."

8

I TOLD HIM you were mine. Natalie, baby girl, consider my claim staked.

He'd told Tilson she was *his?*

That was so…arrogant.

So heavy-handed.

So *hot.*

"Staking claims goes both ways." She looped her arms around his neck, bringing them into intimate full-body contact. God, this was such a very, very bad idea, but he felt so very, very good against her. "We have something in common because I don't like to share, either." She'd seen the women at the racetrack swarm him.

"Done." One step forward and he pinned her to the wall. He bent his head. His cheek nearly touched hers, his hair tickled against her skin as he commanded softly in her ear, his breath warm against her skin, "Now, say it."

She could barely think with the hard wall behind her and the hard wall of man in front of her. "Say what?"

Beau sifted one hand through her hair. "I told you

you'd ask me to kiss you." He traced the line from her ear to her jaw with the bridge of his nose, his breath deliciously hot against her neck. He was slowly, well, maybe not so slowly, driving her out of her mind. "So, ask for it."

She thought not. "If you want it, take it," she challenged him, "but I'm not *asking* for anything."

An almost imperceptible shift of his hips against hers brought his erection in direct contact between her thighs. "Do you always make things so hard?" he said.

"I'm flattered." She rubbed against him.

"You make me crazy." He groaned, resting his forehead against hers. "You have from the first moment I saw you."

It was gratifying to know she wasn't in this emotional-physical morass of self-destruction alone. "Yet another thing in common."

With a tenderness that melted her from the inside out and made her grateful for the support of the wall and his body, he brushed butterfly kisses over her eyelids, down her nose, his mouth finally coming to claim hers. Hot, strong, his lips did exactly what he'd promised— staked his claim. From the sweet, fleeting press of that well-shaped mouth against her eyelids to the devouring of her lips, every kiss proclaimed *his, his, his.*

She'd been kissed and she'd kissed, but never, not even with him last night, anything like this. She ached. She resonated with need. Every inch of her craved every inch of him.

She didn't want to want him. Wrong man. Wrong situation. But it simply didn't matter.

He kissed and felt like homemade sin. She moaned into his mouth and he answered her with a groan as their tongues mated. She slid her hands over his shoulders—she'd never seen or felt such broad shoulders—and was further turned on by the bunching play of muscle and sinew beneath her fingertips and palms. She tugged his shirt loose from his jeans at the same time he delved beneath her shirt hem.

The faint scrape of those calluses he'd pointed out earlier, along with the totally masculine feel of skin over taut muscle, nearly sent her over the top. He insinuated one leg between her thighs as if he intuitively knew her knees weren't quite capable of doing their job. In a moment of instant decision, she grabbed his shirt by the hem and tugged it up.

Beau laughed low and husky, breaking their kiss to finish taking it off. "Baby girl, I like it when Naughty Natalie comes out to play."

She leaned her head against the wall and devoured him with her eyes and her hands. She felt punch-drunk on lust. Pride, circumspection, any scrap of inhibition or reason, all became meaningless. "You have no idea."

She leaned into him and kissed the hair-roughed wall of his chest. His shudder reverberated against her, through her. She found and lapped at his flat male nipple, teasing her tongue against the eraser-tip point, inhaling the scent of his skin, of him. His heart hammered beneath her splayed hand, and his breath came in a ragged draw, much like her own.

"Natalie…baby…"

In a haze of touching and kissing, they moved, stumbling into the front room, which boasted a couch. Lit only by the hall light, she vaguely registered the room and furniture as those in Cash's video. In one swift move, Beau tugged and tossed the dust cover aside. He sank to the couch and she went down after him, straddling him, seating his erection right against her most needy part. Even through denim and underwear, it felt so good she moaned aloud.

He swooped in and captured the moan with his mouth. Long seconds later, cool air kissed her skin as he worked her shirt up.

"You are definitely, one hundred percent overdressed," Beau said with a toe-curling smile. "Let me take care of that for you." He tugged her shirt over her head.

"Because you're helpful that way?" she asked.

He tossed the shirt aside. Even in the shadowy light she saw appreciation glittering in his eyes. "I like to do my part."

She ought to be nervous. He was gorgeous and women flocked around him, and God knows, while she was okay in the face and body department, her boobs were real, there was a sag factor and she was carrying some extra pounds around the middle. Instead, excitement and pure sexual arousal doused any sparks of self-consciousness. And the room's semi-darkness didn't hurt, either.

She was on the verge of spontaneous combustion. "A regular Boy Scout."

He slid his hands up her sides, seemingly unperturbed by the curves, and she closed her eyes, savoring his touch. "I was never a Boy Scout," he said, his voice low and husky.

She still had on most of her clothes. They should stop. She should stop. She should crawl right off his lap, put her shirt back on and go about her business of scraping paint and planning weddings. Except *should* didn't go far when his arousal was nestled against her mound, her skin was absorbing his scent and he'd just unhooked her bra.

She opened her eyes and teased him with a moue of feigned disappointment. "Hmm. Too bad. I always had a thing for Boy Scouts."

He slid her bra off, and his swift intake of breath and the surge of his cock against her as he looked at her bare breasts stoked her own fire. He circled one pouting nipple with his fingertip. "Screw the Boy Scouts."

"Well, I actually never—" His finger grazed her hardened tip and the sensation shot straight to her womb.

"Baby girl, you are about to forget all about Boy Scouts." Before she could blink, she went from on his lap to on her back. He was good.

And then he was on her like a starving man presented with a five-course meal and she was totally, absolutely, officially rendered mindless.

The scrape of his five-o'clock shadow against her neck.

The rasp of his hands on her breasts.

Oh. My. God.

His hot, wet mouth feasting on her nipples.

His nimble fingers delving past her unzipped jeans—when did her jeans get unzipped—into her panties and then, "Oh, yes!" Her cry reverberated off the walls as he dipped his finger into her drenched folds.

"Ba-by girl…you are…so hot…so wet…."

Please… His finger felt so good but it wasn't enough…not nearly enough. A desperate yearning swept through her. She toed off her shoes and shifted her hips up, shucking jeans and panties in record time. He was equally efficient at losing his clothes, but she still beat him to the draw—work boots were apparently a bitch to take off.

She'd seen him wearing nothing more than a towel, but not even *that* had prepared her for *this*. His cock, long, thick and heavy, sprang proudly from a thatch of dark hair. She'd thought it wasn't possible to get any wetter than she already was. She was wrong.

"You've got something for me?" she said.

When had she ever been so bold, so demanding? But when had she ever felt like this? She'd known desire but never this uncontrolled need to have a man, *this* man, inside her. Her vibrator had been a poor, poor substitute last night for what she really wanted. She opened her legs and dragged a finger along her drenched channel in blatant invitation.

His hands were gratifyingly unsteady as he rolled on a condom. His fingers splayed against her thighs, he spread her further and the head of his cock nudged against her nether lips. "Natalie—"

She was somewhere past waiting. She thrust up, taking him into her body. Yes, yes, yes. More.

A low keening burst from his throat. He drove into her, hard and fast. She arched up against him, welcoming him. They both paused, as if of one accord, her eyes locked with his, and she savored the stretch of her body to accommodate the fullness of him, the tight fit of him inside her, as if they'd been custom-made for one another. It was as if his heartbeat became hers, her breath became his, two separate parts merging to make a whole.

He grasped her thighs in his big hands and lifted her. Instinctively she wrapped her legs around him, pulling him deeper, harder still inside her.

Moving in tandem, she met his thrusts. Yes. Over and over and over, the sensations notching her higher and higher and higher. Beau, his eyes glittering, his features etched tight and hot, reached between them and found her clit, pushing her over the edge and plunging behind her as she free fell through waves of pleasure.

BEAU CAME BACK into the room after cleaning up and collapsed onto his back, bringing Natalie with him.

Her heart pounded against him, echoing his own frantic tattoo, and her hair spilled across his chest and shoulder. He'd known, somewhere down the line, they'd wind up in bed together but he really hadn't planned on this now.

"That was…" He searched for the right word.

"A mistake," she supplied, her voice muffled by his chest, her words vibrating against him.

"Hell, no. I was trying to decide between *fantastic* and *incredible*." Well, damn. Her take on it actually suited his overall purpose of driving her away, but in the gratification department he found he didn't like being considered a *mistake*. "That felt like a mistake to you?" He lay there and absorbed the feel of her skin against his, the press of her breasts against his bare chest. He idly smoothed his hand over the silky skin of her bare bottom. She immediately quivered against him and pressed her crotch into his. "Mistake, my ass."

Her soft laugh tickled the hair on his chest and she crossed her hands beneath her chin to look at him. She literally took his breath away. Her hair was a sexy mess and her lips were kiss-swollen. "It's a mistake from the standpoint that you and I shouldn't be doing this. I never mix business with pleasure—" at least she was categorizing them as pleasure "—and I'm not in the habit of jumping into bed—"

He captured a curl around his finger. "Then you're fine because this isn't a bed."

She rolled her eyes at him. "You know what I mean."

"Do you think I don't know that? Do you think I didn't know that from the moment you burst into my toter home on one heel? And tell me we didn't both know from that very second that we were going to wind up here together."

"But you're not my type."

Goddamn but he was getting tired of her hammering home that he wasn't what she wanted in a man. However, come to think of it… "You're not my type, either."

"Then how'd this happen?"

The efficient, everything-on-a-schedule wedding planner looked so adorably bewildered and confounded he had to chuckle. "Well, technically, I'm not sure if it started with that kiss or with the clothes coming off." He followed the indent of her spine down the smooth slope of her back with his hands. "Did you think about me last night after you left? I thought about you. I thought about calling someone to hook up with but that didn't work because I wanted you."

A pleased smile curved her lips. "You could have called me."

He explored the dimples at the top of her buttocks and the crease that bisected her lovely ass. He found he wanted to explore, to learn, to touch and taste every inch of her, which was something of a new experience for him. Typically, he had a good time, he made sure the woman had a good time, and that was that. With Natalie, he wanted to linger.

"We both know that wouldn't have got me anywhere. And you never answered my question." He cupped one cheek in each hand and kneaded. "Did you think about me when you left last night?"

She looked down as if suddenly fascinated by his chest. "Yes." She glanced back up and locked gazes with him. She rimmed her upper lip with the tip of her tongue. "I was wet all night."

Her frankness both surprised and delighted him. It also got the full attention of his dick. His phoenix was rising.

"Did you touch yourself?" he asked, teasing one finger against her from behind.

"Of course I did. Did you?"

"Uh-huh."

He'd started it, and she was laying it on the line. He found the whole conversation hot as hell.

How far would she take the conversation?

"Tell me about it," he said. "Tell me about touching yourself."

She deliberately licked her finger and then traced his nipple with the wet tip. She laughed softly as the contact hummed through his body and sent his cock into full erection against her. "You just want me to talk dirty to you."

"There is that," he said with a grin. "Guilty as

charged." He sobered. "But I really, really want to know what you did."

She levered up to a sitting position. "Put on a condom."

For once, he made short order of following directions, his hands not quite steady. She was unlike any woman he'd ever known before. He felt this need to be part of her, as if when he was joined with her, he was something more than just him.

And then all reflective thought evaporated as she slid her tight wet channel down on his cock, seating him deep inside her. "You were going to tell me about touching yourself," he prompted while he could still talk.

She paused and canted her head to one side as if in deep consideration. "I don't know…."

She-devil. She wasn't being shy, she was toying with him. "You know you want to tell me."

She rocked against him. "I don't know anything of the sort."

He cupped her breasts in his hands and rolled her nipples between his fingers. "C'mon, baby. Tell me."

Well, she was right. He did want her to talk dirty to him.

Her voice was low and sultry as she began to describe touching herself in graphic detail, using all the words men liked to hear and women were sometimes reluctant to say, accompanying her story with a slow ride up and down his dick.

Sweet and hot, and he gritted his teeth to keep from coming. "At this rate I'm never going to get the baseboards finished," she said with a teasing smile, sliding her slick folds along his length.

"Later." He grasped her hips and lifted her. "It's story time now."

"Where was I?"

"The good part…"

She sank back down on his erection, and he felt as if he'd just been hit with a shot of nitrous.

"Which was the good part?" she asked with a wickedly sensual smile.

Beau groaned and thrust up on her down stroke, eliciting a gasp of pleasure from her. "It's all the good part, so just start talking."

9

THE MUSIC of the cicadas filled the night when Natalie and Beau stepped out of the house. A sliver of a moon peeked over the tree line and a breeze whispered through the trees. His hand rested on her hip, and she was aware of the heat from his splayed fingers even through her clothes. The hallway light spilled out of the front door, leaving the rest of the night darker than ever.

He insisted on walking her to her car, and it hadn't gone unnoticed on her part that he'd held the door open for her on the way out of the house. She turned to face him, loath to open her car door and have the harsh dome light ruin the night's soft, velvety darkness.

He brushed his fingers over her jaw. "Do you want to give me five minutes to pick everything up here so you can at least follow me back to Dahlia or even Nashville?" he offered. "It's pretty dark and these country roads can be confusing."

Without thinking, she turned and pressed a kiss to his open hand, the marks of hard work lining his palm.

He was the oddest mixture of man. Arrogant. Infuriating. Thoughtful. His offer weighed in on the thoughtful side but she really needed some distance. She was torn. The truth of the matter was she didn't want to leave at all. She wanted whatever this was tonight to last, to never end. But nothing was static and tomorrow would come, bringing relentless change. So maybe she didn't want to leave but she needed to think, and that didn't include watching his taillights between here and home.

She tried to inject a light note. "Thanks for the offer, but I've never lost my sense of direction due to great sex before. I think it'll be okay." She deliberately stepped away from the heat of his body, when what she really wanted was for him to wrap his arms around her and enfold her like a big, warm blanket. "I guess I'll see you bright and early tomorrow morning."

That was an understatement. She'd have to be up at the crack of dawn to make it back out here by six friggin' thirty. At least she'd be driving against rush hour traffic at that time.

"Wait." As if he'd read her mind, he gathered her close. He was solid and she could get so used to being right here, his heart beating beneath her cheek. "You've got to give me more than that, baby girl," he murmured as he buried his hands in her hair and bent his head.

With a blissful sigh, she wound her arms about his neck and finished pulling his mouth down to hers. His lips and tongue plundered her as if he were a pirate who'd just discovered a treasure chest. And there it was again, that low, insistent throb deep inside her that he awakened so easily. If she was going to leave—and she had to leave—she had to go now. She dragged herself away from him. "I have to go."

He scrubbed his hand through his hair, his face inscrutable in the dark. "I know."

"You know we've got to get some work done in the morning," she said, struggling to remind them both why she was here in the first place.

Even in the dark, she glimpsed his slow, knowing smile and it sent a rush through her all over again. They both knew work would come afterwards. "Then how about six-fifteen instead of six-thirty?"

Never mind, she'd be up well before dawn. And if she was crawling out of bed at four-thirty, they ought to at least make it worth both of their time. "How about six?"

She opened the car door and the dome light was more like a beacon.

"Six works." Another slow smile that tied her up in knots of anticipation. She got in and buckled up. Beau leaned in and brushed a kiss over her forehead. "Drive safe."

He closed her door and tapped on the window, reminding her to lock the doors. It was a testimony to her willpower that she didn't look back at him as she drove down the oak-lined driveway.

She didn't relax until she reached the main road and turned out of Belle Terre's entrance. She still couldn't quite believe Beau had declared her his. Both annoying and a turn-on—much like the man himself.

The dark country roads twisted and turned and she focused exclusively on driving until she reached the stop sign where she picked up the highway to the interstate. She dialed Cynthia.

"Natalie! I thought you were never going to call. I want to hear all about your enforced bondage but first I've got a surprise for you. Are you sitting down?"

"I'm driving." She put on her blinker and merged into the right lane.

"Oh, right. Guess who dropped by the shop today looking for you."

She couldn't think of any appointments she'd had today that she might've missed or even anyone she'd met as a prospective wedding client. Unless it was the cute little blonde, Alex Morgan, that she'd met…was it only last night? "Alex Morgan?"

"Who's Alex Morgan?"

So much for that guess. "A prospect and obviously not who came by."

"Try Shad Jackson. Looking for you."

Shadwell Jackson III. Newest junior partner at Jackson, Burns and Liswick Law Offices. Numero Uno contender, in her book, for the Prince Charming role. "Oh."

"That's all you can come up with? Oh?"

"Maybe he got engaged and wants me to handle the wedding."

"Or maybe he said he hoped you could make a cocktail party with him next Thursday night. He said he wanted to get on your calendar before anyone else beat him to the punch. I penciled him in." Cynthia sounded as if she was bouncing up and down, which she had a tendency to do when she was excited.

Natalie, however, wanted to bang her head against the steering wheel. Damn it all to hell…and back. Why now? Why not a month from now, when she and Beau Stillwell weren't, in all probability, still setting the sheets afire? Hadn't they just had a discussion, of sorts, about staking claims and not sharing? Beau wouldn't be happy if she was going out with Shad next Thursday, the same way she wouldn't be happy if he took one of those silicone-breasted Barbies to that burger joint, Headlights. The other option was to pull out of whatever it was they'd started before next week…and she just didn't know if she had the will-power to do that…not yet, anyway.

"Hello? Oddly enough this silence does not strike me as the 'I'm-so-excited variety.' What's up, Natalie?"

She still wore Beau's scent on her skin, the taste of him against her tongue, the feel of him imprinted on her cellular memory. She swallowed hard. "I can't go with Shad then."

"Look. I know how important financial stability and independence is to you. I know the Stillwell-Vickers gig is the break you've been looking for to put you on the high-end wedding planner map, but you work so hard. Go have a little fun. Don't worry about the repair thing at Belle Terre. God knows, I don't have anything going on after regular hours. I'll cover you on that. I can fill in at Belle Terre with Beau Stillwell next Thursday. Heck, I probably know as much about renovation as you do."

A possessiveness Natalie didn't even know was in her rushed to the forefront. Over her dead body. "I don't think so."

"Natalie? What's going on? Exactly what happened tonight?"

"Exactly isn't important, but I can't go with Shad."

"You didn't…you did. You made out with Beau Stillwell again."

Natalie laughed weakly.

"Jumping Jehoshaphat. You did more than make out, didn't you? You slept with him?"

"It was the best sex I've ever had." Granted she was sure he'd logged in lots and lots of practice, but still… And she didn't consider it kissing and telling if she was being complimentary about him in bed. "But go ahead and tell me how unprofessional that was because it was. Terribly. But, my God, it was great."

"Confession time. I did an Internet search on him after you left this morning. You know, since he races I thought there would be pictures. There were. He's gorgeous, Natalie." Yes. She was ashamed of the sentiment, but double hell, no way was she letting Cynthia anywhere near Beau. She quite seriously had no intention of sharing. "Not your usual type—certainly nothing like Shad, but the man has sexy down to an art. If he decided he wanted you, I'm not sure that even supergluing your legs shut would have done any good."

Natalie laughed again, and even she picked up on the faint note of near-hysteria. "Ouch. You know you come up with some gross imagery."

"Whatever. Look. Caitlyn's not going to freak out because you have a fling with her brother. It's probably a much shorter list of women who haven't or at least wanted to. And he's got love 'em and leave 'em written all over him. You're looking at a couple of weeks, tops a month. Enjoy it. Best sex of your life? How often does that happen? Go for it, but for God's sake, don't do something crazy like tell Shad you're seeing someone else. Just put him off for a while. You're busy, another commitment, that kind of thing. Heck, he probably came around because you didn't show up at the museum opening on Friday night. You can thank Beau for Shad going on the offensive."

Her head was spinning, emotionally she was a jumbled mess, and none of this was par for her course. "I bet Shad was a Boy Scout. And I bet he doesn't have any calluses." Funny how neither notion was as appealing as it had been three hours ago.

"Huh?"

"Never mind. Don't you think that's kind of...I don't know...not right to string them both along?"

"Then dump Beau because Shad's the safe one of the two."

Cynthia was absolutely right, even if she might have some subconscious, vested interest in Natalie foregoing Beau. The only safe aspect to Beau was the certainty that whatever they had was temporary. Prince Charming was always safe and Beau was no Prince Charming. Wasn't that part of the appeal of the whole Prince Charming persona? "You're right." But even now, when she should be totally sated, was totally sated, 6:00 a.m. felt like a lifetime away. "I'll dump him…a little later."

"Natalie—"

Another call clicked in on Call Waiting. Beau's name and number flashed up. "Look, he's on the other line. I'll see you in the morning after I've finished up at Belle Terre." She didn't wait for Cynthia to reply before clicking over to the other line. "Hi."

"Hi," he returned the greeting. One word, single syllable, and he sent shivers skittering over her skin. "I wanted to let you know…for in the morning…"

Dammit. She just passed her exit. "Yes?"

"I like my coffee black."

If he thought for a minute she was fetching him coffee… "Good. Make sure you order it that way."

His laughter exploded on the other end. "I knew you'd say something like that."

Now that she knew he was teasing, well, it had been pretty funny. She teased back. "Are you saying I'm predictable?"

"Not at all." His voice dropped to an intimate note and she knew he was thinking about her recounting her self-gratification while she rode him to an orgasm. "You're full of surprises. I was calling because I didn't know whether you'd rather have a cheese Danish in the morning or a blueberry muffin. Pammy's Petals makes the best stuff you ever put in your mouth."

She had the distinct feeling that he'd turn out to be the best thing she ever put in her mouth but she kept that thought to herself. "You're bringing breakfast?"

"No, baby girl, you're bringing breakfast. I'm just bringing the snack for afterwards."

Six o'clock couldn't come soon enough…and neither could she. "In that case, make it a cheese Danish. And pick up a small container of extra icing. I've got a sweet tooth."

AT FIVE-FORTY, Beau pulled up in front of Belle Terre. The impending sunrise brushed the horizon in shades of pink and orange. Was Natalie admiring the same thing? He knew a momentary pang of guilt that he had manipulated her schedule to wear her out. She couldn't have gotten home before ten last night, and chances were she hadn't dropped right into bed when she walked through the door.

He shook off his twinge of conscience and hauled out the quilt and the goodies from Pammy's. He'd make it worth Natalie's while.

He'd stayed later than he'd planned last night, checking out the fireplace in the front room—a building inspector had given it a good-to-go clearance but he'd wanted to make sure himself—and laying in wood for a fire. Belle Terre had come fully furnished, right down to the firewood stacked out back.

He struck a match to the kindling and spread the quilt on the large wool rug a safe distance from the snapping and popping fire, one of the benefits of seasoned wood. He placed the bag from Pammy's at one corner of the blanket and double-checked his jeans pocket. A four-strip of condoms? Check. Four was doubtful, but hey, even though he was no Boy Scout, better to be prepared.

He realized with a start that the unusual feeling in the pit of his stomach was nerves. When had he ever been nervous like this? He always wanted women to have a good time, to leave satisfied, but now, he realized with a start, he found he really wanted Natalie to walk through the door and be surprised. He wanted to earn a spontaneous smile of pleasure. And, he also realized, he was so damn sick and tired of her I'd-never-go-out-with-you-because-you're-not-my-type song that he wanted to teach her another verse. But, and it was a big but, he didn't want her to fall for him. That would be messy and sticky and that was why he pretty much stayed away from women like Natalie.

And…she was here…or else Tilson had pulled in, and if that was the case, Tilson could pull out pronto. Nope, it was Natalie's van. He watched from the window as she got out of her vehicle. She was wearing a coat. Good thing he'd built a fire to take off the chill in the tall-ceilinged room. She rounded the front of the van. Wait. That was a trench coat belted around her waist. A good look with those high heels, but when had the forecast changed to rain?

Dammit. He had two roofing crews scheduled today and if it rained, he was screwed. He double-checked the sky. Clear. It didn't look like rain but apparently Natalie knew something he didn't. What was he going to do with six guys he couldn't work today who depended on him to get in hours to feed their families? Goddammit, he should've done a late-night weather check instead of thinking about how he could please Natalie. He'd never lost his work focus like this.

The front door opened and closed and the tap-tap-tap of her high heels petered out on an air of uncertainty. "Beau?"

"In here," he said, trying to set aside the worry of how to keep two crews busy on a rainy day. He supposed he could haul them out here, but then that would put this project on schedule, which was precisely what he *didn't* want to happen.

She appeared in the doorway and he didn't have to work to summon a smile, especially when she saw the fire with the quilt spread before it. "Lovely," she said, her brown eyes widening with delight.

"No. I'm looking at lovely." Where had that come from? He never said stuff like that, but it had been a spontaneous reaction to…her. She was beyond lovely.

"Thank you." She crossed the room, her hips swaying beneath that raincoat, her legs bare and shapely in red heels. She stood between the fireplace and the quilt. "I need help with some decisions. I couldn't make up my mind this morning."

"I'm your man."

"For starters, the hair. Up or—" she reached up and pulled out a clip, sending her hair tumbling about her shoulders in a sexy tangle with a small shake of her head "—down?"

His throat went dry. "Down," he managed in a rasp. "Definitely down."

A secretive smile played about her lips. "Down it is." She tossed the clip to the floor. "Next—" she untied the sash with nimble fingers and started working the buttons free on her double-breasted trench coat "—the coat. On or—" she finished the last button and opened her coat "—off."

For a few long seconds he stood rooted to the spot, transfixed. Naked. Gloriously, hotly, sexily, erotically, totally naked. "Off. Definitely off. But keep on the shoes."

"I had a feeling you'd say that."

"Predictable?"

"Not totally." Her glanced flickered to the fireplace and the quilt on the floor. "Only in a good way."

She shrugged the coat back down her shoulders. "And look who's overdressed now."

Before he forgot and had to scramble for them later, he pulled out the condom strips and tossed them to the quilt's edge.

She raised an eyebrow? "Four? You must be a morning person."

"I'm trying to make up for my lack of formal Boy Scout training by always being prepared."

"Hmm." She let the raincoat fall to the floor and knelt at the edge of the blanket to open the bakery bag. "Did they have extra frosting?"

He was rock-hard already and she was worried about what he'd brought from the bakery. "Yeah. I bought one cream cheese and one vanilla."

"Which is your favorite?" she asked, hefting a lidded cup in each hand.

"Definitely cream cheese."

"Okay, then." She put the vanilla back in the bag.

He leaned down and unlaced his boots and then hopped from one foot to the other, taking off his boots and socks. He was going to have to find other footwear as long as Natalie was around.

"Yum. Still nice and warm and gooey." He looked up and damn near fell over. She was on her back, propped on one arm. She held the container of cream cheese frosting in the other hand. She'd coated her nipples in icing and was pouring a small trail down her belly and over first one hip and then the other.

Steadfastly ignoring him, she dipped a finger in the cup and raised her right leg in the air, smearing a generous helping from ankle to knee and then knee to inner thigh. He silently watched, taking off his clothes, while she repeated it on the other leg. He damn near lost it when she tilted her hips upward, drizzled it between her open thighs, and gasped as the warm icing found its target. She finally seemed to notice he was still in the room.

She dipped her finger once again in the frosting and brought it to her mouth. She deliberately licked the white glob off her finger with her pink tongue. She leaned back on both elbows, wearing red heels, cream-cheese frosting and an inviting smile. "Breakfast is served. I hope you like it hot, sticky and sweet."

10

"IF THAT WAS BREAKFAST, it boggles my mind to think what you'd turn out for a four-course dinner," Beau said with a smirk that turned her insides all wonky.

She ignored the wonky feeling and diligently scraped away, having cleaned up and changed into jeans and a T-shirt. "Don't sidetrack me. I've got to get this section finished before I leave this morning." However, she wasn't above shooting him a sideways glance from beneath her lashes and tacking on, "And that Danish was incredibly good."

He returned her look from where he was cutting lumber on a table saw in the corner. "I told you it was the best thing you'd ever put in your mouth."

Instinctively she dropped her gaze to the crotch of his jeans. "Second-best thing."

"Look at me again that way and you can forget all about finishing that section," he said with a mock growl.

He so easily tied her up in knots inside, it was gratifying to know she held the same power over him. She laughed. "Okay. I'll be good."

"Oh, you were very, very good." His low, seductive

voice sent a shiver through her that had nothing to do with the room's temperature. "That's the problem."

"It didn't seem like a problem earlier."

"It wasn't before. It's just now when you're insisting on actually working."

Lord, but he was great for her ego…actually, the way he'd licked and sucked every bit of icing off every bit of her, he was great for a lot of things. And if she had a remote prayer of finishing this section of scraping, she would not think about his clever tongue swirling that icing off her hoo-ha. It was much more prudent to focus on the food itself rather than the sex. "The Danish came from Pammy's? Is all of her stuff that quality?"

Beau nodded. "Her cakes are even better. Pammy did the cake for Caitlyn's college graduation. The woman can bake like nobody's business."

Natalie swatted away the instant flicker of jealousy his comment provoked. For all she knew, Pammy was married with six kids and a husband at home. And he'd complimented her baking, not her prowess in the bedroom. Natalie obviously needed more sleep than she'd got last night if she was going to react so ridiculously to such an innocuous comment.

"Caitlyn wants her to handle the wedding cake, the groom's cake and the reception pastries," she said. "I needed to stop by and wanted to sample something so this worked out well." She knew he was playing her by having her scrape baseboards. And in turn, she'd played him by making a production of being on her knees with her butt in the air. But she still hadn't figured out exactly what was behind this game he was playing. "Look, I'm seriously worried about scheduling and getting all of this done in the time frame we're looking at."

He shrugged. "Construction and remodel can be iffy. It's not unusual to have to adjust time lines."

"That's fine." He obviously wasn't too concerned but she was—enough for both of them. "But we don't have a lot of room to play with. Their schedule is tight. That's why I'm here."

He made a calm-down gesture with his hands. "I don't have a race this weekend so I'll be working out here if you're available."

She couldn't read him. Was he asking whether she was available for sex or whether she was available to scrape baseboards? "Cynthia, my assistant, can handle the rehearsal and dinner on Friday evening." They often traded duties. Both of them seldom needed to be in the same place at the same time. Saturday's wedding was Natalie's, however. "I have a wedding on Saturday. It'll be late, and by the time the day is over I don't think I'd be a whole lot of help anyway."

That slow, suggestive smile that sent a furrow of heat through her belly curved his mouth. "It sounds as if you'd probably need your feet rubbed on Saturday night." And oh, my, he had that sexy drawl down to an art form.

Hard as it was to turn him down, she knew she'd be tired, and driving under those conditions didn't seem wise. "I don't think I'd be up for driving to Dahlia. This wedding is going to be exhausting."

"My truck knows how to get to the big city." Despite his smile and teasing words, his eyes were serious.

This was notching things up a level. It was one thing to fool around at Belle Terre, where she wouldn't return once the wedding was over, and a totally different animal altogether to have him at her place, in her bed. Did she want him there? In about two seconds she came up with a resounding *yes*. And who knew how long whatever they had going on would last? Anything burning this hot was sure to burn out equally fast. "My feet would be a good place to start."

"How about I bring dinner? If you like Thai, I could pick some up on my way in. There's a good Thai restaurant off I-40."

"I've never had Thai." It was a bit of a surprise that he had. She'd sort of slotted him as a meat and potatoes kind of guy.

"I could bring something else."

"No. I'd like to broaden my horizons and try something different."

"Mild or spicy?"

He was serious and it was crazy the way her heart was racing over the prospect of him showing up with dinner and a foot rub. "Definitely spicy. I like chicken. I prefer noodles over rice. Beyond that, surprise me."

He glanced at her coat folded by the door and quirked his lips into a pulse-pounding smile. "Don't expect me to show up wearing just a trench coat. I'm not looking to be arrested. By the way, you drove all the way from Nashville wearing just that coat and those heels?"

She laughed. "No. I stopped at the convenience store right before you get off the highway and changed in the bathroom."

Beau offered a quick nod of approval. "Resourceful."

"I try."

"What time should I be there?"

"Eight would be good if you can wait that long to eat."

"Eight would be perfect. I just need your address. I can pull the directions off MapQuest." He felt in his pocket and then looked around. "Damn. I've misplaced my BlackBerry."

He retraced his steps into the front room. She got up from her cramped position on the floor and helped him check under the sofa, beneath the coffee table and the arm chair.

"Do you have it set on ring tone or vibrate?" Natalie said.

"Ring tone."

"Okay, hold on a sec and I'll call you." She grabbed her phone and scrolled down to his name.

Within seconds AC/DC's "Highway to Hell" began to play from beneath the quilt's edge. What… "Is that your general ring tone or is that special for me?"

He grinned, crinkling the corners of his eyes, and she had her answer even before he uttered a confirming word. "I thought you deserved your own."

She couldn't contain her laughter. She reclaimed her spot on the floor and picked up the scraper. "'Highway to Hell'? I'm not sure whether I'm flattered or insulted." Which was patently untrue. It was funny, and they both knew it. There was a spot by the floor that just wasn't coming off. Or was that a nick in the wood. She leaned down to see better.

"I meant it in the best way possible. And you know I don't spend a buck to buy a ring tone for just anyone."

"Yeah? 'Highway to Hell' certainly makes me feel special." She glanced at him over her shoulder and realized he was somewhat mesmerized by her extreme on-her-knees position. Bad idea that it was, she nonetheless gave a little wiggle with her tush.

Two strides and he'd closed the gap between them. He stood behind her and she could practically feel the heat radiating from him, the sexual waves vibrating between them. "Everybody's different. Cream-cheese icing makes me feel special."

He hooked an arm around her waist and hauled her up, wrapping his arms around her from behind. She sighed and tilted her head to one side when his lips found the sensitive spot behind her right ear.

She offered a token protest. "I'm never going to get this baseboard finished." Even as she said it, she wiggled her bottom against the burgeoning bulge behind her, feeling the onslaught of wet heat between her thighs that was ever present when he was within touching distance. She let the scraper fall to the floor once again and curled her hand around the sinewy bulge of his bicep. The scent of arousal clung to them.

He chuckled as he nuzzled her neck and unbuttoned her jeans, working down the zipper. Her muscles tightened in anticipation of his touch. "Of course you will…just not this morning."

BEAU PARKED in the alley behind his mother's shop and used the back door. There was no point in going through the front, and besides, there was something kind of emasculating about walking through the door of a store with dresses and nightgowns in the front window. When his mama summoned him to her place of business he was a backdoor kind of guy—even though he was proud as punch of her.

He waited in the back until her customers cleared out. She greeted him with her customary hug and kiss on the cheek. He couldn't remember a single time from the day his father had died that his mother hadn't had a hug and kiss for him when he saw her.

She cocked her head to one side and studied him, pursing her lips. "Something about you looks different. Did you get a haircut?"

He ran his hand over his head. "No haircut. Maybe it's just the spring air." Ha. Maybe it was Natalie and the great sex, but that was hardly the thing a guy said to his mother. Even if he was thirty-two.

She merely quirked an eyebrow as if to say she didn't believe in the restorative power of a spring day, but wisely didn't press any further.

"You needed me?"

His mother, one of the original steel magnolias suddenly looked as nervous as a cat on the proverbial hot tin roof.

"I wanted to talk to you about something. I wanted to mention it to you before I talked to Caitlyn. I'd rather you hear it from me first. I mean, I've always felt as if we could talk about anything—well, within reason."

"Mom, you can discuss anything with me."

She drew a deep breath and said in a rush, "How would you feel about me dating? I mean, I think it's been a suitably decent interval since your father passed, and both you and Caitlyn are adults now and, well, how would you feel about that?"

All that on an exhale. "I think the first thing you should do is breathe before you pass out and mess up your hairdo."

His mother smiled and gratefully picked up his thread of silliness. "Well, Lila's right next door if I need a touch-up."

That had been one of the main appeals for his mother in locating her shop here. She was right next door to her best friend's hair and nail salon. And the same clientele frequented both.

"You're a grown woman and I've always thought you had great judgment—well, maybe not the time you made me clean all the toilets in the house for a month because I lied about my book report in fifth grade, but other than that you've had a good head on your shoulders." She swatted at him and he ducked before wrapping his arm around her shoulders. "I want you to be happy, and if going on a date makes you happy, then I want you to go on a date."

"You don't think I'm too old?"

"You're kidding, right?"

"That's reassuring." She beamed a smile of relief. "I didn't want to say yes or no until I'd talked to both you and your sister. Natalie said she thought y'all would be okay with it."

"You talked to Natalie about this?" Was it just in his head or was she beginning to insinuate herself in the fabric of his life? Planning his sister's wedding—which was, in fact, her job. Playing confidante to his mother. Blowing his mind...and various and sundry body parts.

"She was here doing some shopping and the timing was just right. She's such a sweetie. Good head on her shoulders. Pretty, too." She gave him a pointed look. "How're the renovations at Belle Terre going?"

"It's slow going."

"Why'd you really want her to help you out there?"

"Well, as you just pointed out, she's smart, easy on the eyes, and I needed help."

That made his mother laugh.

"I'm honored you talked to me about this," he said, getting back to her dating. "There's just a couple of things I'd like to cover with you before I leave, though." He clearly recalled the "talk" she'd had with him shortly before his eighteenth birthday. Bless her heart, she'd spoken to him as if he was still an untried boy, unaware that he'd been having sex since he was fifteen. One of the cheerleaders had initiated him into the pleasures of someone bringing him to climax rather than his hand. He managed to keep a straight face. "Dating is one thing, but I'd prefer not to wind up with a little brother or sister."

Bright red flooded her face. "I'm past that—" She stuttered to a halt. "You knew that. You're just teasing me."

"It'd sure be the talk of the town."

"Your daddy had that same sense of humor."

"I know. But I'm not him." He'd made damn sure of it. *He'd* never leave the people he was supposed to care about the most in the world destitute. *He'd* never seek his out in the bottom of a whiskey bottle.

He supposed he could thank his father for teaching those lessons by negative example. He was a better man for it, but he was still mad as hell that his mother and sister had suffered. And it galled him that his mother still mourned the man who'd put his love of gambling and Jack Daniel's before her. His father didn't deserve her loyalty or her love.

"I know you're not, son." She looked beyond him,

as if looking at him was too painful. "You try so hard… I've never known whether to tell you or not, but I'm thinking maybe I should."

"Tell me what?" This didn't sound good at all.

"Your father…he had problems, Beau."

He'd thought she was going to tell him something he didn't already know, something he hadn't spent sixteen years trying to fix. "No kidding."

She suddenly looked every bit her age and weary beyond words. "Your daddy was a manic-depressive." She exhaled a long breath as if she'd handed over a heavy weight. "It was an illness, Beau. A mental illness. That's how we wound up so in debt. When he'd cycle down, he'd spend money we didn't have. And the alcohol just made it all worse."

His chest felt tight. "Why are you telling me this?"

"Because you need to know. It's past due, but it's just always been easier not to mention it." She drew an unsteady breath. "It's hard to admit mental illness in your family." Her eyes grew wistful. "He was so much fun when we first met, when we first married. And Lord, he was so proud of you." She looked at Beau. "He was sick, son. It was as if he had a cancer, but it was a mental cancer."

Oddly enough, that did put a different spin on things. Beau had assumed his father had made irresponsible choices, but if an illness was driving him, how much had actually been choice? He realized his chest didn't feel nearly as tight, and the tension that had been coiled deep inside him for sixteen years didn't feel quite as intense. "All the more reason for you to be happy now. So, just make sure you practice safe sex, Ma," he said on a teasing note. She hated being called Ma.

"Beauregard Jameson Stillwell, you're not too old for…well, I guess you are, but…."

"S'okay, Ma. I'll behave. And I guess I need to head out 'cause it sounds like I better go home and clean my shotgun…just in case."

She laughed and pretended exasperation. "You're a mess."

"I've been told it's part of my charm." He dropped a kiss on the top of her head and headed for the door. Whoa. He'd totally dropped the ball. He stopped and turned. "Wait a sec. Before I go home and start polishing my rifle, when are you going out, where are you going and, more importantly, who are you going with?"

"Well, I haven't said yes yet, so I don't know when or where. But Milton Lewis asked me out."

"Milton? You mean, Scooter?"

His mother sniffed. "I prefer to call him Milton, seeing as how that's his given name."

Scooter wanted to go out with his mother? Suddenly his comment about safe sex wasn't so damn funny. Neither was his crack about his mother having a baby. Not a damn bit funny. Not that there was anything wrong with Scooter, but this was a whole different ball game now that her suitor was actually someone he knew. Not just someone he knew but, damn…Scooter.

"Now you're scowling. You don't approve of Milton? You've spent nearly every weekend with him for the past seventeen years at the racetrack. Is there something I should know about him?"

"Nooo. Scooter's a nice enough guy…it's just…I never…well, I guess I never thought about him wanting to go out with you."

"Why? What's wrong with me? Do you think I look too old?"

Shit. He was making a mess of this. "No. Not at all. What I meant, I guess, was I never thought that you'd want to go out with Scooter."

"Why? Is he a womanizer? A playboy at the track?"

Scooter a womanizer? Good thing Beau wasn't eating or drinking because he would've choked. Obviously his mother saw Scooter in a whole different light. "Not hardly. He's a motorhead. I guess I just don't see him as your type."

"He's a nice man and he's always had a good sense of humor."

He was also only about an inch taller than Beverly and as bow-legged as the day was long. However, he was a good guy, and Beau was ninety-nine percent certain Scooter would treat his mother like a lady. At least, he'd better.

"You're right," he said. "I can't think of a reason why you shouldn't go out with him."

Except he didn't want to see his mother get hurt any more than he wanted to see Caitlyn make a mistake with Cash Vickers. But then again, Caitlyn had sounded so damned happy when he'd talked to her.

Beau had had no idea the extent of his father's problems. He hadn't had a clue that Scooter wanted to ask his mother out. He'd set out to get Natalie to quit, and now he couldn't wait to see her again.

Life as he knew it was going to hell in a handbasket all around him.

11

SATURDAY EVENING, Natalie gave a small sigh of satisfaction as the shaving-cream-adorned car carrying the bride and groom disappeared around the corner. Shanna Connors and Mark Tippens were heading to the Ritz-Carlton for the night and then catching a flight Sunday morning for a week of honeymooning in Bermuda.

"Good luck to him," Cynthia murmured at her elbow.

They stood apart from the guests, who had begun to drift back to the reception hall, others heading toward their cars.

Natalie exchanged looks with her assistant. She knew exactly what Cynthia meant. *High-maintenance* didn't begin to describe Shanna and her mother. Mark would need to grow a set of steel balls to deal with those two, and unfortunately, she didn't think he was in the steel-ball-growing business.

"How long?" Cynthia asked. Natalie had developed a nearly unerring knack for knowing which couples would and wouldn't make it.

"Two, three years tops." She eased one foot out of

her shoe and flexed it. She hoped Beau was serious about that foot rub. Her feet were killing her. "It'll take that long for him to work up the courage to leave."

Cynthia nodded. "Yep. Hey, I'll wrap up things here," she offered. "You head on home."

Natalie didn't understand it but Cynthia's favorite part of the whole process was tying up all the loose ends—making sure the cake top was boxed up and delivered to wherever the bride specified, getting the wedding dress to the cleaners and looking after the myriad other after-details that Natalie found so tedious. "Are you sure? I know you like that stuff but you'll have to deal with…" She let her words peter out, stopping short of calling Shanna's mother by name. Cynthia knew precisely who she meant.

"Not a problem."

"Then I'll gladly take you up on your offer."

They walked in tandem toward the parking lot. "You look beat," Cynthia said, more by way of concern than criticism.

"Thanks, that's reassuring. It's been a tiring week."

Getting up every morning at four-thirty and then not getting to bed until nearly midnight was exhausting…but worth it. She still hadn't finished scraping the foyer baseboard.

Sex was a great way to start and end a day, and as depraved as it might sound, the time in between dragged. And she was in a bad way because she'd been out to Belle Terre yesterday morning, but last night and today had been out of the question with the demanding Shanna and her mother.

A day and a half and she missed Beau Stillwell like crazy. Alarmingly, not just the sex but *him*—his arrogant, breath-stealing smile, his sense of humor, his take on world politics, which didn't necessarily coincide with hers but was well-thought-out nonetheless. And it was sheer madness because she'd been busy, busy, busy with wedding details, but missing him had been there still.

Cynthia's teasing smile held a wistfulness. "I'd tell you to get some rest but I think rest isn't on either your or his agenda. Go. Have fun. I've got this covered."

Cynthia was worth her weight in gold. Yet another reason to do a great job with the Stillwell-Vickers wedding, other than the fact they were one of the most in-love couples she'd ever worked with. When she got the resulting surge in business, the first place she was putting some of that money was in a raise for Cynthia. Natalie knew things had to be tight for her since her sorry jackass of a boyfriend had moved out. Cynthia didn't complain, but she was now footing all of her bills on her own. Plus, she flat-out deserved a raise.

If Natalie had any sense remaining, she'd call Beau and cancel. She'd go home, take a warm bath and crawl into bed alone for a good night's sleep. But all her sense had deserted her because to her way of thinking, there'd be plenty of nights to crawl into bed alone in the near future.

But not tonight.

BEAU SHIFTED the flowers, wine and small gift bag to his left hand and grabbed the handle of the shopping bag containing their dinner. Goddamn but he was nervous. He'd damn near licked every inch of the woman at some time or another in the last five days and she'd returned the favor, so why the hell his heart was pounding like some kid was beyond him.

Maybe it was because up until now when he'd seen her he'd been in his world. The drag strip, Headlights, Belle Terre. Now he was entering her turf. And he had to admit he was out to prove a point. Damn her, she'd wounded his masculine pride when she'd told him she wouldn't go out with him if he asked her—not that he'd planned on asking her at the time. True, he didn't have a college degree and he worked with his hands, but he wasn't going to be shortchanged. He could stand up to any accountant or attorney. Of course, in all fairness to her, he had come off as something of an asshole.

He'd parked in the delivery alley behind her place, next to her van. He couldn't say he particularly liked the idea of her parking back here when she got in late…and he'd made sure she got in late all last week. This wasn't a bad section of town, but it was a damn alley. He didn't like it, didn't like it even a little bit.

His step faltered as he considered that she could've been mugged…or worse. He was going to have to re-think his strategy of dragging her out to Dahlia to wear her out, because if something happened to her because he'd kept her out late, he'd have to bust some heads, starting with whoever dared to touch her and ending with his own for putting her in that position in the first place. And maybe he'd look up Black Jack, Alex Morgan's cop fiancé, and ask him to swing by this area more often or have one of his buddies check up on Natalie. If she lived in Dahlia, it'd be a different story. Outside of the drug ring that Drew Fisk had been running out of the drag strip, Dahlia was crime-free for the most part.

He rang a delivery buzzer at the back door. She'd told him her business was downstairs, and much like shopkeepers used to do, she lived upstairs. It made sense to roll two rents into one, even if it left her with-out a lot of neighbors to rely on.

Within a minute or two he heard her throwing the locks on the other side. She opened the door. "Hi," she said.

It was as if all the air in his lungs took a hike.

"You are beautiful, baby girl." He said the first thing that came to mind when he finally managed to breathe.

Her hair was piled on top of her head with tendrils framing her face, as if she'd just climbed out of a bath. She smelled fresh and warm, and her skin looked dewy soft against a black V-necked sweater and black slacks.

"Thank you. You clean up pretty nicely yourself," she said.

He'd traded the jeans, T-shirt and work boots for khakis, loafers and a blue golf shirt his mother had given him for Christmas because she said it matched his eyes. "Thanks."

"So, come on in. The stairs are this way."

"Would you mind showing me your shop first?" He wanted to see what she did, the place where she worked.

"Sure." It didn't take long because her shop was fairly small. She had as much stockroom as storefront. She carried an assortment of wedding paraphernalia—guest books, feathered pens, white gloves, champagne glasses and an extensive assortment of veils.

"Nice," he said, indicating the wall of veils.

"They're all one of a kind. I sell them on consignment. And that's it."

He nodded. The place looked like her. "It's warm and inviting, but elegant."

She dipped her head. "Thank you. So, you're probably starving. Come on and I'll show you upstairs."

He followed her through the stockroom to a set of narrow, steep stairs. If his hands hadn't been full, he would've never been able to keep them off her delectable ass as she climbed the stairs ahead of him. Her apartment door stood open at the top. He stepped in behind her and she reached around him to close the door. He caught a whiff of her perfume and fresh scent.

"So, this is it. Nothing fancy but, for now, it's home. Decorated via early American thrift store." It was neat and tidy and, yes, obviously done on a budget. She chattered on, leading him into a small, damn near minuscule kitchen. He was pretty sure she was as nervous as he'd been when he arrived. "And the kitchen, as you can probably figure out, is this way." She took the take out bag and placed it on the counter. "Thanks for picking up dinner." She plucked the flowers out of his hand and put them next to the food. "And the flowers are beautiful. I'll have to find a vase." She looked from the wine bottle to the refrigerator to him. "Should I chill the wine?"

His attention wasn't on the wine. "I don't care. I missed you."

He reached for her, and she flew into his arms. "Oh, God, me, too."

And then they were tangled up in one another. He pressed kisses over her eyes, her hair, her chin, her mouth. She devoured him the same way, both of them murmuring almost incoherently between kisses and hands beneath clothes.

"Felt like forever…"

"Thought tonight would never come…"

"…need you…"

"…desperate…now…"

Scattering discarded clothes along the way, Beau found himself with the press of her mattress behind his knees. Natalie pulled back the comforter and sheet with one tug and pushed him to the bed, following him down. He sank into the soft feather mattress, the sheets cool beneath him, Natalie soft and, oh, so hot on top of him.

He rolled her to her back, pinning her arms over her head, and pressed hungry, openmouthed kisses down her neck, over her breasts, her belly, tasting the satin of her skin against his lips and tongue, until she was writhing beneath him and he was on the verge of losing control.

"Beau…please…" she gasped.

It felt as if it took forever for him to roll on his condom, his movements frantic and jerky with the need to be inside her. One thrust and his groan joined her wail as her silky slick channel welcomed him home. And in that one thrust, in that second of being buried so deep inside her the head of his dick nudged her womb, the near explosive franticness left him. Her lovely eyes widened and he felt the same sense of rightness, of peace settle through her.

An ache, a foreign humility filled his chest. He was honored to be here, in her bed, in her body. How the hell had he gotten so lucky? His Natalie, his baby girl.

"You are so very, very beautiful," he said softly as he began to make love to her, to pay homage, to offer his gratitude for what she was sharing with him. Slow, sweeping strokes that echoed that initial sweet homecoming.

"You are the most beautiful man I've ever seen."

Women had told him they liked the way he looked. He'd heard any number of compliments before, but they had all seemed superficial. However, with Natalie, there was nothing superficial about it...and it wasn't *him,* it was *them.*

"We're beautiful together," he said. "Look." He glanced down at where they were joined. "Me inside you. You around me. That's beautiful."

She looked at where his cock was buried inside her and her eyes were smoky when her gaze tangled with his. "Yes, it is." Slowly, deliberately, maddeningly, she canted her hips, taking him that much deeper inside her wonderland.

Beau lost track of everything except the feel of her hot, tight channel wrapped around him, the taste of her tongue in his mouth, the soft mewling sound she made in the back of her throat, the uneven rhythm of their mingled breaths, the scent of her, of them... He felt the first tremor go through her.

"Come for me, Natalie."

"No." She clenched her muscles around his cock as her orgasm began to roll through her. "I'll come *with* you."

And it was as if a storm roared through him and ripped him free of a weight that had anchored him, and in the aftermath of his climax he floated free, buoyant in her arms.

12

NATALIE LOVED the way Beau lay sprawled in her bed, as if he belonged there. She propped herself up on one arm and shamelessly admired the broad expanse of his chest with its smattering of dark masculine hair that gave way to trim hips. It was the body of a man who worked hard every day, who earned that flat, tight belly and those cut biceps by doing his job. He was hot and he was here and that's where she wanted him to stay.

"I don't want you to go," she said.

Beau turned his dark head on her pillow and looked at her, his blue eyes sated, content. "I don't want to go."

"Then stay." It was an invitation, not a plea.

He caught her hand up in his, threading his fingers through hers, offering that slow, sexy smile that robbed her of coherent thought. "If I'd known it was a spend-the-night party, I would've brought my pajamas."

She looked over his nakedness, slowly, deliberately, and offered her own smile. "It's okay. You won't need them. Do you really wear pajamas?"

"No. Not since I moved out on my own. Want to sleep in matching outfits?" This time he was the one to let his gaze slide over her. "His and hers?"

"Sometimes you're positively brilliant."

He grinned and her belly tightened. For long seconds she simply absorbed the feel of his fingers against her hand, the scent of their lovemaking mingled with the smell of her freshly laundered sheets, the devastating sexiness of him in her bed.

"Natalie…" He broke the moment, his tone more serious. "I don't want you helping on the renovations anymore."

Her heart picked up its pace and not in a good way. "But the schedule's already tight. I may not be that much help, but I've actually got a good bit done." *And when will I see you again if I'm not seeing you twice a day? Was he already tired of her? Was this letting her down easy? The beginning of the big dump?*

"I'll figure something out but I don't like you getting back late at night and parking in that damn alley." A scowl drew his dark eyebrows together. "And then it's dark when you leave in the mornings. I don't like it. I'll figure something out on the renovations."

She was so relieved he wasn't pulling the plug on them, whatever they were now, that she laughed aloud. "I'm fine. I carry pepper spray on my key chain and this isn't a high crime area."

"Baby girl, if anyone hurt you, laid a finger on you,

someone would be dead and I'd be rotting in jail because I'd kill the son of a bitch."

She swallowed hard. He meant it. Every word. She fully believed he'd do extreme bodily harm on her behalf. With her peace-love-and-happiness-to-all background she should have found the possessiveness, the threat of violence alarming. Instead, it made her feel cherished, something she'd never experienced before. Something warm and tender unfurled inside her.

"Beau, that's so sweet—"

He interrupted her. "No, it's not. It's not sweet. It's self-preservation. I'm being a selfish bastard. I don't want to go to jail and I don't want to have to kill anyone."

There wasn't even a glimmer of humor lightening the intensity of his eyes. He was one hundred percent serious. "I'm telling you, I'm not in any danger," she said.

"Not anymore, because you're not going to be getting back here after eleven o'clock. It's just not worth it. End of discussion."

Okay, his charm had just worn thin. "End of discussion?" She untangled her hand from his and sat up, pulling the sheet over her lap. "I don't think so. And it's not up to you to decide whether it's worth it or not. News flash—I'm not yours to manage."

He knifed up, as well, but didn't bother with the sheet. "Goddammit, Natalie, my sister getting married at Belle Terre in a couple of months isn't worth you putting yourself at risk. Caitlyn can just wait on that wedding if she has to."

"Goddammit back atcha, Beau." Who did he think he was? "Don't you get it? Don't you understand anything? Your sister is going to marry Cash one way or the other. I've seen a lot of couples in the last three years and I've got a great radar going as to who'll make it and who won't. The wedding I did today, I give them three years together at best. But Caitlyn and Cash—what they have is real and it's deep. They're both in it for the long haul."

His expression remained hard and set. He just wasn't hearing her.

"For God's sake," she went on, "the man bought her a plantation house because she wanted it. Because he wanted to give her a dream. Yeah, he's a rising star, he's on his way up, but he doesn't have that kind of money just lying around. If you don't have Belle Terre ready and I don't do my job, then you and I have robbed her of a dream."

"You really believe that?"

"I really *know* that." Maybe he was starting to get it, to understand. "And I've got dreams. You're smart. You've got to know that orchestrating the wedding Caitlyn wants will make my career." He was a businessman. He worked for himself. Surely he could relate to this. "Short-term, it'll mean I can give my assistant the raise she desperately needs and definitely has earned. In the long run, it means I turn this into additional retail space and buy a small house I can call my own. I grew up never having a thing that was all my own. This is my apartment but I share it with my business. Sue me if wanting financial stability and my own home is a sin."

He crossed his arms over his chest in an are-you-finally-through gesture and she totally lost it. No! She wasn't through yet.

"So, do not tell me what something is or is not worth to me. And for god's sake, don't sit in *my* bed, in *my* apartment, and tell me a damn discussion is over. Nobody crowned you king here."

The bedroom was so quiet she heard the hum of the refrigerator all the way from the kitchen. She waited, fully expecting him to get up and stomp out. If that was the way it went, so be it. She didn't care how good they were in bed together or how much she'd missed him in one lousy day and a half, he wasn't going to dictate to her. He might run his mother's and sister's lives, but he didn't run hers.

He sat there, his expression closed, inscrutable. Finally, he nodded, one curt up-and-down. "Okay. Points taken. The discussion is obviously not closed. Will you give me a few days to figure things out, during which period of time you will not, in my estimation, put yourself at risk by coming and going so early and so late?"

She'd fully expected him to storm out. She took a deep breath. He was still here and he'd made what she figured were huge concessions for him. And she realized, rather sheepishly, that she'd once again lost her temper with him, which was so unlike her, and been extremely profane, also unlike her, in the interim.

"I'll agree to that," she said. "And I'm sorry I lost my temper. I'm really not usually like that. You just seem to have this effect on me."

Beau chuckled and it was a relief to feel the tension between them dissipating. "Hot-wiring." He relaxed against the pillows propped against the white iron headboard.

"What?"

"Hot-wiring. It was one of the first things I learned to do with a car when I was a kid. You see a car you like and you don't have the key, so you just bypass the system. If you hot-wire it, you can take what you want. You hot-wire it and the ride is yours."

"Isn't that illegal?"

"Yeah." He smirked. "But I'm damn good at it. And I hate to break it to you, baby girl, but I've hot-wired you."

"You wish," she shot back.

"No, baby, I know."

"Has anyone ever mentioned you're arrogant?"

He pretended to ponder for a moment. "Nope."

"Consider it mentioned, then."

He wrapped an arm around her and pulled her onto his lap. "You know, I think we just had our first fight."

"No. I'd say our first fight was the first time we met."

"Okay. I'll give you that. But we just had our first *naked* fight."

"Do you always have to argue everything?"

"No. But I will argue that we just had a fight and now that means we need to make up." He dipped his head and nuzzled along her collarbone, sending all the right signals to all her right parts.

She dropped her head back, allowing him full access, and murmured. "As I mentioned before, you do have occasional, brief flashes of brilliance."

He stopped. Why'd he stop?

"Hold that thought, but for now, I really need you to argue with me."

"And that would be because…why?"

His smile sent a hot promise all the way through her. "Because then I'd have to tie you to the bed to make a point and have my evil, wicked way with your body."

The mere thought, the mention slicked her. She moistened her lip with her tongue, feeling all hot and bothered and breathless. "You wouldn't dare."

His eyes dared her. "Try me."

"We did not just have a fight. We do not need to make up. And you will not tie me to this bed and tease me to the point of madness before you have your evil, wicked way with me and screw me mindless."

"There you go. You've left me no choice. Now I have to tie you up and screw you mindless or you'll consider me a Boy Scout."

"What can I say? A man's got to do what a man's got to do."

And she knew just the man for the job.

BEAU WATCHED in fascination as the morning sun slanted through the bedroom blinds, illuminating Natalie's face. He thought he could watch her forever without getting tired. He'd been awake for an hour now, memorizing the curve of her brow, the arch of her lips, the slope of her nose.

Watching her sleep had given him lots of think time. He'd entertained the thought that maybe he was wrong about Cash and Caitlyn. The thought that even if he wasn't wrong, it was ultimately Caitlyn's decision and not his. And perhaps, the most important realization of all…that he could watch Natalie Bridges sleep for a very long time, perhaps a lifetime, and never grow tired of the show.

Natalie chose that moment to flutter open sleep-heavy eyes. Sexy right down to the very breath she drew. His sex drew its own deep breath, swelling with the influx of oxygen and the woman next to him.

"Morning, baby girl."

She gave a lazy stretch. "Morning. Did you sleep okay?"

"Great."

She snuggled into his side. "Have you been up long?"

"Awake for a while." He glanced down at his hardening cock. "Up, just now."

"I hope you didn't just lie here because you were afraid you'd wake me. I sleep like the dead. A habit I developed early on with the constant influx of kids in our house."

He knew that for a fact because he'd actually gotten up and done the bathroom ritual, complete with brushing his teeth—she'd rustled up an unopened two-pack last night—and then climbed back in bed with her.

He trailed a finger down her nose. "I was just enjoying the view."

She smiled and rolled to the edge of the bed. "Hit the Pause button, I've got to go to the bathroom."

He watched her cross the room naked, admiring the curve of her back, the indent of her waist, those legs that were so adept at wrapping around his waist or draping over his shoulder, and, best of all, the sway of her bottom. "The view just gets better and better," he called out as she walked out of the room.

She laughed over her shoulder. "Pause, big boy, pause."

Funny how the room seemed a little less bright, a little less warm without her in it.

He'd been so focused on her, he really looked at the room for the first time. The walls were a pale pink with white lace curtains flanking the one window. There wasn't much room for anything other than the white iron bed, a round nightstand and a mirrored dresser. It was uncluttered and intensely feminine, just like the woman herself.

Natalie waltzed back in, wearing a smile, her glistening breasts with their pert pink nipples and the triangle of dark hair between her thighs issuing a mating call to his dick.

She stopped at the foot of the bed on his side. A wicked little smile curved her mouth and glinted in her eyes. Oh, yeah. That look always meant good things were about to happen. Natalie climbed onto the mattress, between his legs and up his body, her hands and mouth stopping for sampling detours along the way, her hair a silken tease against him. She crawled all the way up him and then went back to the part of his anatomy that was throbbing with excitement and need.

She scattered teasing kisses along his thighs, hips, and below his navel until he was ready to beg her to touch his…finally. Her mouth on his cock sent a warm tingle rushing through him.

"Mouthwash," she said, shooting him a sassy smile. "Minty fresh."

She took her breasts in her hands, put them together and slid them down over the head of his cock. They were soft and pillowy and warm and slick and felt so good he groaned aloud. "Oh, baby."

"Ah, you do like it."

"*Like* would be an understatement. Is that oil?"

"Uh-huh. We both need a shower anyway so I thought now was the perfect time for things to get messy."

Messy was good. "Oh, yeah."

She rolled onto her back and looked at him through half-closed eyes as she palmed her oil-slicked breasts and tugged on her nipples until they were rosy and distended. She gathered her creamy globes in hand and pressed them together. She pushed her breasts up, leaned her head down and slowly, erotically tongued her nipple, and he thought his cock might explode then and there.

"You are every man's wet dream come to life. A lady in the street—"

She interrupted him with a laugh. "And a whore in bed? I try. So, climb on and make a mess."

13

BEAU LEANED AGAINST the kitchen counter and watched Natalie upend the leftover coffee into the drain, her short silk robe clinging to the rounded curve of her hips.

"I've been thinking—"

"I hope you didn't strain anything," she tossed over her shoulder with a smirk.

"Smart-ass." He smacked her butt playfully.

"Umm…" She made a little purring noise in the back of her throat. "Don't start something you don't have time to finish."

Well. "Does that mean I need to turn you over my knee one day?"

"Possibly. But right now I've got to get dressed." She settled the glass carafe back in the coffeemaker and dried her hands. "I told my mother I'd get out there today to share the love with Miguel."

That's right. Her new foster brother. She'd taken the call at Belle Terre. "Are you kicking me to the curb?"

It was only a few steps from the kitchen to her bedroom.

"Yes. Or you could come with me if you wanted to and we could go to Belle Terre afterward to get some work done."

"Damn. I think you may be more of a workaholic than I am." He shrugged into his shirt. Natalie had been right. Hanging his clothes in the bathroom during his shower had steamed most of the wrinkles out.

"No." He found it quirky and sort of endearing that she modestly turned her back to him to slip on her panties and bra. "I've just got a mission and that's to see your sister enjoy the wedding of her dreams." She opened the closet door and sorted through hangers. "And I'll make sure I leave in time to get back at a decent hour. I can be very determined."

He grinned, thinking back to her standing in the middle of his toter home telling him to kiss her ass. "No kidding. You tracked me down at the racetrack. Nightmare Natalie. Stubborn is more like it."

"Because you wouldn't cooperate and call me back," she said, her voice muffled by the clothes. "And my determination is simply one of my many endearing qualities." She slipped a sundress over her head and worked the back zipper up.

"Need some help with that?" he offered.

"I've got it."

He took over regardless, tugging the zip the rest of the way up. "I can't say *endearing* came to mind the first time I met you." He trailed a finger over her shoulder.

"Thanks." She tugged the dress down over her

hips. "Ha. You don't even want to know what came to mind when I met you."

"'Kiss my ass' was, I believe, the choice phrase that came from those luscious lips of yours." He finished tucking his shirt into his pants. "Do you need to check with your mother first before I just show up?"

Natalie laughed, picking her brush up from the dresser. "Er, no. One more warm body in the house won't faze her in the least. She'll probably just try to adopt you." He sat on the edge of the bed and watched her brush her hair. She looked at him in the mirror. "Be strong and just say no. Seriously, they're great. They're warm and loving but they are chronically disorganized. I'm a throwback in the gene pool. I'm telling you, it's mayhem there." She put the brush down and gathered her hair into a loose ponytail at the nape of her neck, fastening it with a long barrette. "You'll see." She turned to him as she clipped on silver hoop earrings. "And way back when, you were about to share a thought."

There was something intimately satisfying in watching her get ready. "Yeah, before I was so rudely interrupted."

She sniffed and stuck her nose in the air. Beau laughed at her theatrics. Underneath those prim suits she wore, his woman was a little on the crazy side. He liked it. "So, I was thinking about it and you know real estate's a helluva lot cheaper in Dahlia than Nashville."

She nodded and turned to the mirror once again, but she was listening. She picked up a tube of mascara or eye shadow or whatever the hell it was that women put on their faces.

He continued, "Even factoring in the costs of commuting, you'd still come out ahead." He'd worked it all out while he'd watched her sleep this morning. "And I happen to know a guy in construction who could work you a deal on remodeling this for retail space. For that matter, he could probably build you a house at close to cost. It'd take some finagling with his schedule, but once race season ended in November, his weekends would be free again."

He couldn't read her expression as she looked at him in the mirror. "And why would that guy in construction do that for me?"

"Because Dahlia's a hell of a lot safer than Nashville. That guy in construction is basically a self-serving bastard. He'd sleep a whole lot easier at night if you were tucked in your own little house in Dahlia." And he didn't want to examine it too much closer than that.

She brushed a soft pink gloss over her lips and turned to face him again. "But then I'd be beholden to that guy and I don't like being beholden to anyone."

Absolutely, breathtakingly lovely.

"You know, we have more in common than you realize. And you wouldn't be beholden to anyone. Just think about it."

She nodded. "I'll think about it."

That had at least gone a whole lot better than when he'd broached the subject of her not working at Belle Terre anymore. He didn't need her working at Belle Terre anymore, because as of this morning, he'd decided to pull all his crews out there.

Caitlyn would have her wedding on time.

NATALIE BOLTED the rear alley door behind them and then double-checked it. Beau's paranoia was catching. His truck was parked behind her van. It seemed a silly waste to take two vehicles.

"Did you ever fix that seat belt in your truck?" The sun was warm against her shoulders and back. It was a beautiful day. By all rights, she should've had another wedding today but the couple had cancelled when the bride succumbed to a case of cold feet a week and a half ago. Natalie and Cynthia had handled that, as well. It didn't happen often, but it did happen. And it had left her with today open.

"No." He shrugged. "Too many other things going on this week."

She rounded the van to the driver's side. "Then I'll drive. Plus, I know the way."

He folded himself into the passenger seat. "Control issues."

He was so good at making her laugh...when he wasn't busy pissing her off. "Whatever. Just buckle up."

She put the key in the ignition and turned it. *Click,*

click, click. That so did not sound good. She looked at Mr. Motor in the seat next to her.

"Baby girl, I believe your starter is history."

He was speaking a foreign language. "Is that bad?"

"It's not good."

She resisted the urge to bang her head against the steering wheel. "Can you fix it?"

"If I had some tools and a floor jack." He ran his hand over his stubbled jaw. "It's a whole lot easier to just lift it."

"I have no idea what you just said."

"Give me a minute or two and I'll hook you up." He climbed out of the van and paced on the sidewalk while he made phone calls on his cell. She sat in the van and mentally went over the bills she had due the next couple of weeks and what her cash flow should be.

Five minutes later, he opened the passenger door and leaned in, bracing his arms on the door frame. "I've got you taken care of. We're going to tow your van out to Scooter's and he's going to fix the starter. I'll drop you off at his place to pick it up late this afternoon. In the meantime, I'll drive us out to your folks."

She didn't want to come across as ungrateful but her budget was so tight it squeaked. "How much is the tow going to cost?"

"I did a little work for Darren Thompson, the guy with the tow truck, last year. He was short on cash at the time so we worked it out on trade. He owes me.

He said he'd be right out to pick it up. It's a freebie. And he'll flatbed it."

She didn't know what flatbedding it was but apparently it was good. It sounded sort of sexual, if you asked her, but then again, when she was around Beau, everything sounded sort of sexual. And she couldn't let him trade out a tow he'd worked for.

"But that's a debt he owes you, not me."

"Natalie, don't worry about it." There was a faint edge of exasperation to his voice. He really was used to being in charge. "You're actually doing him and me a favor. I never need a tow and he's just glad he can do this. It gives him the chance to pay up."

Fine. She gave up on that. "Well, what should I pay Scooter? He's doing this on a Sunday afternoon."

"You're actually doing Scooter a favor, too. He's had too much time on his hands the last couple of years since Emma Jean died. Replacing your starter gives him something to do and makes him feel useful. Plus, he likes you."

He had it all worked out. "I know what you're doing." He was taking care of her. The same way he took care of his mother and his sister. And he was doing it without her having to dip into her wallet.

"The only thing I'm doing is giving you a ride out to your folks and then to pick up your car. Pull the ignition key off and leave it under the floor mat. It's not as if anyone can steal it anyway."

She detached the key, slipping it beneath the mat,

opened her door and climbed out. "Uh-huh. You're fixing things." Heavy-handed. Arrogant. Sweet.

He grinned, totally unrepentant. "Put it down to early adolescent training." Beau opened the truck door on his side and offered a slight bow. "Your carriage awaits."

She laughed as she slid in ahead of him to the center seat, her heart beating a little faster. The seat right next to him. The one with a functioning seat belt. He climbed in behind her. His warmth and his scent seemed to enfold her. He was big, solid, sexy…and, for right now, hers.

His fingers grazed her hip when he fastened his seat belt, and her breath caught in her throat.

"Okay, where are we going?" he said after he cranked the truck.

"We need to head north on 65. Do you know how to get there from here?" She had no idea how familiar he was or wasn't with Nashville.

"Yeah. I've got it."

A few blocks later, they approached the expressway ramp. For all that she'd seen him drive like a bat out of hell down the racetrack, he was a very careful driver on the street.

She couldn't remember if Beverly had said his age or not. And if she had, Natalie didn't remember, so she asked him what had been niggling at her as he drove through the city. "Your mother said you kept the family afloat after your father died. You were how old?"

It was almost imperceptible but his face tightened and she could swear his body tensed next to her. "I turned sixteen two days after we buried him. The bank repossessed our house two weeks later. I promised him I'd take care of my mother and my sister." Another deceptively casual shrug of those broad shoulders that had taken on the weight of the world at an age when most boys were mainly concerned with a Saturday-night date. "I take promises seriously."

He made a right onto the ramp and merged into the northbound traffic.

"You're a complicated man," she mused aloud.

"No, I'm not. There's nothing complicated about me. I keep telling you, I'm ultimately a selfish bastard. I made a promise. If I don't keep it, then I feel bad about myself. Bottom line, I do what I have to do to feel good about me. Self-preservation."

"If you say so."

"I say so," he said.

He wasn't what she'd thought she wanted. He wasn't what she'd been looking for, but she could so easily fall in love with him. Heaven help her, she was already more than halfway there.

BEAU HAD TO ADMIT to being shell-shocked a couple of hours later when they left Natalie's parents' farm. "You're right. That was crazy. Cool, but crazy. It must've driven you insane."

"See, now you know what happened to me. Early-childhood-induced madness, hence my need for my own space and everything nicely scheduled and organized. I'm telling you, they were born in the wrong decade because they're hippies."

"They seem devoted to one another."

"Always. They met at Berkeley in the Seventies. What are the odds that two people from just outside of Nashville, Tennessee, would find one another in a liberal arts school in California?"

"How'd they wind up back here?"

"I think they envisioned themselves as being part of some Foxfire-like element."

He had no idea what Foxfire was, but he wasn't about to ask. He'd Google it when he got home. "You look like your mother. You're both beautiful women." It was like seeing what Natalie would look like in twenty years. Still beautiful. The notion gave him a funny feeling in his gut.

"Thank you." A sweet blush stained her skin. Amazing. He'd licked cream-cheese icing off her most intimate parts until she'd come and she hadn't blinked an eye, but let him tell her she was beautiful and she was embarrassed.

"You're welcome." Sudden inspiration struck him. "Look, let's skip Belle Terre today. I know you've got a schedule and I swear I'll take care of it, but I want to show you something."

She leered at him and he laughed, sliding his right

arm around her shoulders, steering with one hand on the wheel. "Baby, I'm always ready to show you that."

She snuggled into his side. "I'm always ready to have a look."

Despite her comment and the underlying sexual tension that always seemed to hum between the two of them, a comfortable, content silence stretched out as he navigated the switchbacks that cut through Tenessee's hills.

Half an hour later, he turned onto a dirt road and slowed down at the yellow flag at the edge of the ditch. "See that flag? My property starts there."

He hung a left and drove down the familiar, rough-cut road that wound through a mixture of hardwoods. "About a month ago, the dogwoods and redbuds were in bloom and it was beautiful."

"It's beautiful now."

"Just wait." He so wanted to show her his property. He'd had his eye on it for years and then last year he'd finally had the money to buy it. Now he almost had the money to build his house on it. His piece of paradise, bought and paid for.

He hadn't felt this way in years. He felt like a kid on Christmas Eve—both anxious and excited.

He rounded the curve and crested the hill and the clearing on the top of the ridgeline was there with the Tennessee hills spread out in all their blue-green glory. It was a view that never failed to pierce his soul.

He put the truck in Park and killed the engine.

"Oh." It was all she said. It was all she had to say. She looked up at him and her eyes shimmered with the sheen of tears. She felt it, too. He'd *known* she would get it.

"I know," he said quietly. He opened the door, got out and held out his hand. "Come on."

Natalie put hers in his and slid out on his side. To his way of thinking, he was never going to fix that seat belt.

The young spring grass was soft underfoot as they climbed the slight rise together. "This is where I'm going to build my house."

"It's so beautiful it makes me ache inside."

The sun glinted in her hair, picking out strands of copper and gold. A slight breeze rustled the leaves and swayed the grass. "That's exactly how I feel."

"When are you going to build it?"

"I thought I'd start this fall but it'll more likely be next spring, maybe summer." That was because, as of now, he was pulling all of his work crews off their jobs and sending them to Belle Terre. It'd screw with his cash flow, because all the jobs he pulled them off wouldn't pay until Belle Terre was finished, and it wouldn't be finished for a couple of months now. And he'd also turned the idea of trying to fit in a couple more races and picking up the money there.

But he'd come to the realization that he couldn't continue down the path he'd taken regarding Caitlyn and Cash. If Cash broke her heart, or even dinted it,

Beau would kick his ass to the Tennessee line and back, but marrying him was Caitlyn's choice. And *maybe,* not that he was totally convinced, he *might* have been wrong about Cash. He was willing to entertain the notion that his judgment had been clouded by overprotective instincts.

Both his mother and Natalie seemed to think Cash was okay, and Beau realized both women's opinions held a lot of sway for him. Somewhere in the course of the last week, Natalie had slipped under his skin, had become more than just a wedding planner to be gotten rid of. He respected her—her intelligence, her work ethic, her independence—and the two of them were explosive in bed together.

Running her ragged by dragging her out to Belle Terre now struck him as a supremely asshole plan. His crews would be there first thing in the morning. "There's been a slight change in plans. A blip on the radar, but nothing I can't handle."

She curled her fingers around his. Her hand felt tiny in his. "Will your house have a front porch?"

"Yep. Got to have a front porch. A back porch, too."

She nodded. "That's good. Porches are important, especially with this view."

"Absolutely. Porches are a Southern institution."

"Where's the front door?"

"Right here." He pretended to open a door. "Ladies first." She tugged on his hand and he followed her inside to where the foyer would be. "Den." He gestured to the open space to his left, still clasping her hand. "Kitchen, bathroom—"

"Show me the bedroom," she interrupted, her tone solemn, sensual.

He led her down the "hall" to the back right corner of the house. "Here," he said, facing the distant hills. "This is what I'll see when I wake up in the morning and what I'll see when I go to bed at night."

"Is this the bed?"

"Yeah, on this wall."

She nodded soberly, her eyes intense, a stillness about her that suited this place. Without looking away from him, she slowly, deliberately reached behind her and slid down the zipper of her sundress and slipped it off, laying it on the grass. She stepped out of her sandals and curled her toes into the green cushion.

His eyes locked on hers, he followed her lead and pulled off his shirt, spreading it on the soft spring grass next to hers. He stepped out of his pants as her underwear joined the other clothes. She stood waiting patiently, expectantly, while he took off his briefs.

Bare, she sank to the bed made of their clothes and stretched her hand out to him.

"Lie down with me."

14

NATALIE DIDN'T TRY to contain her sigh of content-
ment as they headed down the highway once again.

Beau ended his phone call. "Scooter has your van
ready. We can swing by and pick it up and then maybe
grab some dinner."

"Sounds like a plan."

She had never known such absolute, blinding hap-
piness in her life. Of course, she'd never been in love
before, either. It was too late for heaven to help her.
She was done. Toast. History. She was totally, irrevo-
cably in love with Beau Stillwell. What had happened
in the meadow defied description. Their lovemaking
had been as spiritual as it had been physical. She'd
come so close to telling him she loved him then and
there, but it had been so close to perfect that she'd
simply loved him with her body instead.

He looked down at her and smiled and her insides
turned to gooey mush. Lord, she could look at him,
have him look at her that way, for the rest of her life.

"I'm never going to fix that seat belt," he said,
draping his arm over her shoulder, his fingers resting

right above her breast. The scent of their passion clung to his fingers.

"That works for me." *I love you.*

"I think it's supposed to rain on Wednesday." He sent her a boyish grin.

"Um, okay." Talk about a subject change.

"I could pick you up. You could wear that raincoat. You know, so you wouldn't get wet."

She got it now. She liked the way his mind worked. "Uh-huh. I could, couldn't I?"

"Damn. I wish it was going to rain tomorrow." He offered a mournful sigh.

Natalie grinned, shaking her head. "You're crazy."

He stroked his fingers along the edge of her breast. "You make me crazy."

Umm. She loved that husky, low-keyed tone his voice took on when he said things like that. And he made her crazy in a totally good way. "That's a two-way street."

He pressed a quick kiss to her hair and slowed down, putting on his blinker. "Here's Scooter's place," he turned left into a gravel driveway marked by reflective lights on stakes, "and there's your ride all ready to go."

Her van sat in front of a detached garage that was about twice as big as the frame house that sat slightly behind it. Scooter emerged from the shop and greeted them as she and Beau got out of his truck. A large tree—she had no clue what kind…tree identification wasn't her thing—shaded the area.

"Beau. Nat'lie. Got you all fixed up." He gave them a ready smile as he wiped his hands on a worn rag.

It was impossible not to like Scooter. "Thank you so much. What do I owe you?"

"You don't owe me nuthin'." Scooter shoved the rag into his back pocket, shaking his head. "I'm always messing around under one car or another. Might as well have been yours today."

It was a little chilly in the shade with the breeze blowing. Natalie crossed her arms. "But what about the part you put in? You can't pay for that."

Scooter nodded his head toward Beau. "Compliments of Stillwell Motors Racing."

"But—"

"Take it up with the boss there. I just did what the big man asked me to do."

Beau did a lousy job of looking innocent. "You cold? I've got a jacket behind the seat if you want it."

He could be infuriating, but at the core of him, he was a thoughtful man. "I'm okay. Thanks, though. And I will take it up with the boss later." She shifted from one foot to another. It'd been a long time and she'd had a big glass of iced tea just before they'd left her parents' house. And there was something about being chilly that intensified nature's call. She was in desperate need of facilities. "Um, is there a bathroom handy?"

Scooter scratched his head. "You don't wanna use the one here in the shop. It ain't none too clean, but the one in the house is in good shape. Just let yourself in the back door and it's the second door on your left."

"Thanks," she said, already moving in that direction. She had to *go*.

"It was the starter, right?" she heard Beau ask as she rounded the corner of the garage.

"Yeah. And I found a couple of loose belts that I replaced and changed out the spark plugs. I gave it a good going over. It ain't gonna leave her stranded anywhere anytime soon."

She smiled to herself as she crossed the neat lawn and let herself in the back door. In his own arrogant, high-handed way Beau had looked out for her, taken care of her. She could get used to being taken care of that way. Not that it would impugn her independence, but simply to know you had someone special to turn to. To know he had her back, the same as she would gladly have his back.

She let herself into Scooter's house. The kitchen smelled like vegetable soup and the empty can on the counter confirmed that'd been his lunch. A solitary bowl sat in the sink. A wooden sign, with *Emma Jean's Kitchen* written on a rolling pin—the kind you picked up at a country craft fair—was mounted over the doorway leading into the rest of the house. There was an ineffable sadness about the single bowl and the sign, and Natalie wondered if Beverly had agreed to go out with Scooter. She hoped so.

She took quick care of her business and checked

herself in the bathroom mirror while she washed her hands. Good grief, she had grass in her hair and a big grass stain on the back of her dress. Maybe Scooter hadn't noticed. She plucked the grass out of her hair, but there was nothing to be done about the stain. She retraced her route back to the garage. She was still on the side of the garage when she heard Beau.

"I'm fine with you going out with her, I just don't want her to get hurt," he said.

Natalie paused, unsure of what to do. She didn't want to interrupt what was obviously a personal discussion, but then on the other hand she was eavesdropping. She opted to do nothing. It wasn't as if she didn't already know about Beverly and Scooter.

"Beau, you know me well enough to know I'm not going to hurt her."

"Make sure you don't."

She winced at the hard note in his voice. She was pretty sure even the affable Scooter wasn't going to take that well. She understood Beau's protective instincts but he could come across as terribly overbearing sometimes. Of course, that's what made him the man he was—the man she'd fallen in love with.

"Look, I know you made a promise to your daddy. I never thought it was right for him to ask such of a boy, but I know you promised and you've been a man of your word. But you've got to know when to back off some."

Nope. Scooter hadn't taken it well at all.

"You're coming mighty close to crossing a line, Scooter. I'd suggest you back down."

"That ain't gonna happen. And you're one to talk, Beau. Because you've already crossed a line, and somebody has to check you on it and I reckon that somebody's me."

Good grief, it sounded as if they were squaring up. What would she do if one of them threw a punch?

"I haven't crossed any line."

"Yes, you have. Me and the boys know you don't want Caitlyn to marry Cash. I've known you for a long time. I knew from the beginning you thought him buying Belle Terre was a squirrelly thing to do with his money. And I know ain't nobody ever gonna be good enough for your baby sister."

"You through?"

"Nope. Just gettin' started. I understood you not just taking it to her cause that sure wasn't gonna change her mind. And I sorta thought it was funny when you tried to trip that little gal up by not returning her phone calls—" Natalie realized with a start that Scooter was now talking about *her* "—and then trying to get her to quit by wearing her out, dragging her to Belle Terre twice a day." Son of a bitch. She'd known from the beginning he was up to something. The signs had all been there, but she'd chosen to ignore it, bury her head in the sand. "But I saw the grass in her hair and the grass stain on her dress, and you sleeping with Nat'lie to sabotage Caitlyn's wedding—that crosses the damn line."

Oh, God. She braced her hand against the side of the garage as nausea swept over her and she couldn't breathe. How could she have been so stupid? It had all been a sham, a scam. Bile rose in her throat. She would not give him the satisfaction of puking.

"You don't know what you're talking about. This is none of your business."

"I'm making it my business. Somebody's gotta stick up for Nat'lie before you break her heart."

She squared her shoulders, lifted her chin and willed her feet into action, wading in to wage war and fight her own battle.

"Thank you, Scooter." She walked over to Beau and wasn't sure who she surprised more when she slapped him on the face so hard her hand hurt. He didn't even flinch. Dear God, she'd never struck another human being in her life. But she'd never felt as if her soul had just been ripped out of her, either.

How had she ever imagined herself *in love* with him? At least she'd had the good sense not to profess undying devotion. "You are despicable. Loathsome."

At that, he flinched. "Baby gi—"

She would not cry. She let fury roll through her and scorch away the tears. "Never, ever call me that again."

Her handprint was bright red on his cheek. "Natalie, if you'll let me explain what—"

"Ms. Bridges, if you please." She stood ramrod straight. "And what is it exactly that you'd like to explain, Mr. Stillwell? Did Scooter get it wrong? You weren't trying to sabotage the wedding? And it'd be nice if you could manage the truth. If you're capable of the truth."

"The truth. I did set out to sabotage the wedding. Actually, I just wanted to delay it." He scrubbed his hand through his hair. "I don't want to see Caitlyn make a mistake. I worked damn hard to make sure she had stability and some financial security. I'm not sure Cash can give her either one. I figured with enough time, he would either prove himself or shoot himself in the foot. And he likes the women."

The urge to slap him again was so strong she stepped back from him. "And he loves your sister. You know what the problem is? You look at Cash and you see yourself. What? Like you don't like the women? Like they don't throw themselves at you left and right? But here's the difference, Cash loves Caitlyn." She put every ounce of betrayal and anger into a sneer. "I've met the both of you, and Cash Vickers has more integrity in his pinkie than you do in your entire body."

"I know it looks bad but—"

She stopped him with a raised hand and an unamused laugh. "I don't want to hear it. You played me. Plain and simple. Admit it. At least be man enough to own it."

"Okay. I'm owning it. I played you…at first. But dammit, listen to me now. I love you."

She felt as if she were breaking into a million pieces, but she refused to fall apart in front of him.

She laughed again. In his face. "Please. Please don't do this. I'm not really sure what your angle is with that, but I think you've already insulted me enough."

Scooter piped up. "Nat'lie, I've known him since he was running around naked as a yard dog, and I can vouch that he's never told a woman he loved her."

She shot Scooter a pointed look. "Has his sister ever been about to marry someone he disapproves of? See? That's what I thought." She rounded on Beau. "Was I supposed to be so overwhelmed by your skills in bed that I would forget about my job? Or maybe you wanted me to find this out and you thought I'd be so humiliated that I'd quit? Am I supposed to swoon now over your faux declaration of love and be so swept off my feet while you continue to play your manipulative games? Think again. If anything, I'm more determined than ever to see Caitlyn get the wedding she wants. And I told you early on, you're not my type. You're not what I'm looking for in a man."

"I've got three work crews showing up at Belle Terre in the morning," he said quietly.

She clapped, slowly, deliberately insulting. "Bravo. I'll be there to make sure they're doing their job and not just standing around."

"That's not necessary. I said I'd handle it."

It would be bittersweet going out there again but at this point she didn't trust him any further than she could throw him. "What? I'm going to take your word for it? Please. Your word means less than nothing.

Unfortunately, I'll have to see you at the wedding rehearsal and on the day your sister gets married. Other than that, however, I never want to lay eyes on you again. I think you owe me that."

His face took on that hard, set look she'd seen last night. "If that's the way you want it."

"That's definitely the way I want it." She couldn't get home soon enough to wash his scent and his touch off her skin. She walked over to her van and stopped at the door, turning to him. "Oh, and tell your crew I won't be there Friday morning. I have a date on Thursday night—a junior partner in a law firm. I anticipate a late night."

THURSDAY AFTERNOON, Beau straightened from where he was cutting a piece of baseboard that needed replacing when his mother walked through Belle Terre's front door. He'd set his equipment up in the front parlor. Four days into it and he and the guys had made a huge dent in the work. Right now, all the men were gathered outside, breaking for lunch. He didn't care about lunch. He wasn't hungry. And, much as he loved her, he didn't want to deal with his mother right now.

"I don't want to talk about it, Mom," he said, hoping to head her off at the pass.

She gave him her customary hug and kiss. "We're going to talk about it, Beau. Scooter thinks you're angry with him."

He ran a weary hand over his face. He hadn't slept in days. He thought he'd covered this with Scooter but apparently not. "No. I did a stupid thing and it bit me in the ass. In spades. I did this all on my own." He looked at his mother and the sorry-ass truth poured out of him. "I love her."

"That's what Scooter said."

"I took her out to show her my land and…Mom, she got it, she felt it there the same way I do." If he lived to be a hundred, he'd never ever forget making love to her in the grass, the sun warm against their skin, as she unwittingly claimed his soul, and he was glad to give it. In that moment, he'd become hers and he'd claimed her as his for all eternity.

Beverly's eyes widened. "You took her to the house site?"

"Yeah."

Tears gathered in her eyes and she put both arms around him and hugged. "Oh, son," she said, releasing him.

He had no pride left. He bared his soul. "When I'm with her…I don't even know how to describe it."

Understanding, sympathy and pain all glimmered in her eyes. "You don't have to. I loved your father the same way."

For the first time since his father died, mention of him didn't stir a cauldron of anger in Beau. He'd done a little online research and his father had been a classic case of manic depression. And Beau had finally realized that Monroe Stillwell had loved them but he'd been unwell and untreated.

"She said she never wanted to see me again and asked me to stay away. She said I at least owed her that. And she's right."

"I'm sorry, Beau. Give her some time."

He plowed his hand through his hair, jealousy clawing at his soul. "She has a date tonight. An attorney. A junior partner. The very thought is driving me crazy." The thought of her kissing someone else, laughing up at him, touching him, him touching her... It was like pouring acid on an open wound. "Remind me that getting knee-crawling, ass-kicking drunk is a very bad plan."

They both knew what had happened to his father. Beverly shook her head. "That's a disaster in the making."

"I know. And I've already screwed things up enough." Dammit. He just felt so useless doing nothing. Well, technically, he was busting his ass at Belle Terre, but at this point, the ball was in Natalie's court. He'd stated his case. All he could do was wait and pray for a change of heart. Well, actually there was one thing he did need to do. Put it down to stress that it hadn't occurred to him earlier. "I can't change things with Natalie, but I do know one thing I have to do."

15

FRIDAY MORNING, Natalie hurried down the stairs from her apartment. She'd been awake until nearly five and then had drifted off, only to find herself embroiled in a nightmare where she was sinking in quicksand and Beau kept throwing her a rope but she was too stubborn to take it. She'd been glad to wake up. And now she was late and sleep-deprived. Not a stellar start to the day.

"You look like shit," Cynthia observed, foregoing the customary "good morning."

"Thanks," she said on a sarcastic note. She hadn't missed the bags and dark circles under her eyes when she'd looked in the mirror this morning. She didn't need Cynthia to point out the obvious.

Cynthia quirked an eyebrow in inquiry. "How was your date with Shad last night?"

Natalie poured herself a cup of coffee, in desperate need of the caffeine. She settled down at her desk and looked at her day planner rather than her assistant. "I didn't go."

"Natalie! You stood him up?" She'd known Cynthia was going to react this way. "You stood up Shad Jackson III? You know you probably just blew your chances with him."

As if she gave a flying fig about Shad. Her time had been better spent soul-searching. Shad could never hope to be half the man Beau was. She'd been angry and hurt when she'd thrown that out at Beau, when she'd called and accepted Shad's invitation. She'd wanted to wound Beau, she'd wanted him to hurt as she'd hurt. She'd wanted to betray him as she'd felt betrayed. "I don't care. I'm not remotely interested in Shad. Going would've been a waste of his time and my time, and I would've felt even crappier than I already feel."

Cynthia took on a stern expression. "Natalie, you can't give Beau this kind of power over you. Be strong."

She was being strong. Figuring out just who and what her Prince Charming was and wasn't had required fortitude and taking a good hard look at herself. She'd always envisioned her true love to be someone like Shad. Sanitized. Safe. In retrospect, she realized she'd been looking for someone who didn't stir her too deeply, who didn't throw her into a tailspin with just a look. She'd also realized love, real love, wasn't safe at all. It meant opening yourself to hurt and heartache, and it was chaotic and messy.

"What if I was wrong, Cynthia? I was so hurt, so angry, I felt so betrayed…but…I don't know now. His crews are legitimately working. They'll be finished the renovations ahead of schedule. And what did he gain by showing me where he was building his house?" She wanted to cry every time she remembered making love with him there. It had been so tender, so special. How could that not have been real? "He didn't have to offer to help me renovate here and build a house in Dahlia."

Cynthia frowned over her tea mug. "But what if you were right?"

Cynthia was the walking wounded. "But what if I was wrong?"

Their conversation and her personal angst-fest were cut short by the ringing of her cell phone. Caitlyn Stillwell. Natalie squared her shoulders, took a deep breath and answered in her cheeriest professional tone, "Hi, Caitlyn."

"Beau called me last night." Caitlyn, true to form, cut straight to the chase.

She couldn't read Caitlyn's tone. "Really?"

"Yes. Really. The first thing I want to say is this call is strictly personal."

What else could she do but agree? "Okay."

"Beau told me everything. He told me about his reservations, his stupid plan, how you and Mama set him straight. Thank you for going to bat with him on our behalf. It's not easy to go toe to toe with him. He's used to being in charge."

"You're welcome. And I noticed," she tacked on dryly.

Caitlyn laughed on the other end. "I'd love to see you taking him on. He's used to women doing back-flips to please him." Natalie could've lived without that reminder. "Well, everyone but me and Mama." Caitlyn's voice lost its teasing note, grew serious. "He gave us his blessing, Natalie," she said softly.

Tentative hope bloomed in her chest. "That's wonderful. I'm really happy for you."

Caitlyn sniffled on the other end. "You have no idea what this has cost him."

"Then tell me. I want to understand."

"Shortly after Daddy died, our house was foreclosed on." Beau had told her that. "We lost everything. House, furniture, cars. Daddy owed money to anyone and everyone." He hadn't told her that. "We moved in with Nana and Papa, which was pretty much miserable because Nana and Mama never got along. I was so little that I didn't really realize it at the time, but Beau was sixteen and he started driving a race car and winning and he worked at the IGA sweeping floors after school and he saved all that money so that after a year we moved out of Nana and Papa's house and into our own place."

She'd known he'd shouldered a heavy burden, but she'd had no idea it had been that heavy. Caitlyn wasn't through.

"Daddy dying changed him, Natalie. He's never owed a penny to anyone. Everything is paid for in cash. If he owns it, no one can take it away from him. That land he took you to is paid for. And just for the record, he's never taken anyone there other than me and Mama. He's fun, he's got a wicked sense of humor, but he's private. I don't know if you really understand what his taking you there meant. That's not a part of him he shares. And him sending those crews out to Belle Terre—it means he waits another six months to start building his house. He won't start building until the money's in the bank to pay for it. I wish Cash and I had the money to front him, but we don't. Once again, he put his dreams on hold for me."

Natalie took a deep breath, trying to steady her racing pulse, and then she said aloud what her heart had known all along. "I love him."

"Thank God. Now will you please put him out of his misery, because he is miserable."

"That makes two of us."

"Y'all are pathetic." Caitlyn sounded disgusted.

Natalie agreed.

"You're gonna have to step it up to win," Scooter said as Beau levered himself out of the car after the first round qualifying. "You've got to get your head in the race."

"I'll make you a deal. You don't tell me to get my head in the race again, and I won't tell you to get your head out of your ass."

Darnell, Tim and Scooter all exchanged a look which didn't do a damned thing to improve Beau's surly disposition.

"Hey, man, why don't you go check out the ball game in the toter while we check the spark plugs?" Darnell suggested. The three of them exchanged another look.

Screw them. None of them was sitting around with his thumb up his ass while the woman he loved was out with some fancy-schmancy junior attorney who, in all likelihood, had totally screwed up the most important relationship of his life. Fine, he'd go sit on his useless ass in the toter.

He stomped off, knowing full well he was being a dickhead. He wasn't good at waiting, at "giving her space." She'd told him she didn't want to see him, but that was just too damn bad. He didn't believe for a minute that she didn't love him. That day, on his property. He knew what he'd seen in her eyes. She had a temper. She was stubborn as hell. And she was his. He was tired of sitting around like some dickless wonder. He was going to clean up and then he was going to Nashville. He was going to stake his claim for good.

He climbed the steps and slammed the door behind him for good measure. He dropped to the couch and pulled off his racing boots.

Out of nowhere, the pocket door between the kitchen and bathroom slid open. Natalie stood in the doorway, a towel wrapped around her, her hair a sexy curtain across her shoulders. "Can I help you?"

His mouth went dry. Hell, maybe he was hallucinating. God knows, he hadn't slept in days. "Natalie?"

She took a step toward him. "I'm sorry."

He wanted to touch her, take her in his arms, but he wasn't so sure that he could think clearly once he did that, and this was an important conversation. "For what?"

Her brown eyes bared her soul, handed it to him for safekeeping. "For not believing you. I've been so miserable. I love you. You're everything and more a Prince Charming should be."

"Natalie—"

She quieted him with a finger to his lips and just that touch sent heat spiraling through him. "Not Natalie. Say it. Please."

He took a wild guess at what she wanted to hear. "Baby girl."

Finally, he got something right. "You have no idea…"

"I have plenty of idea." And to hell with not touching her. He grabbed the edge of the towel. "Once again you're overdressed for the occasion." He yanked and tossed the towel to the floor and dragged her up hard against him. She was all soft skin and rounded curves and his dick was clamoring for attention. He still had important business to take care of with her. "I love you."

"I know." She smiled and reached between them, fondling him through his pants.

If she kept that up… "I know you know, but I thought it needed repeating."

He kissed the spot below her ear and she shuddered.

"I'll never get tired of hearing it," she said in that hot, breathy voice that fired his pistons. He cupped her buttocks in his hands and picked her up. She wrapped her arms around his neck and her legs around his hips and rocked against him with a wicked little smile playing about her mouth. God, he loved her mouth. He backed her up against the kitchen counter.

One long, hot kiss later he said, "I take it Scooter, Darnell and Tim knew you were in here."

"Uh-huh." She licked at the base of his neck. "I got here after you were already in the staging lanes. Tim brought me to the toter. Are you through racing for the day?"

"Uh-huh. What'd you have in mind?"

She ground her mound against him. "I've never done it with a guy in a racing suit."

He ground back. "I can help you with that."

"I've also never done it in a toter." She nipped at his jaw.

"We could kill two birds with one stone."

She batted her brown eyes at him. "Or we could do it twice."

"I like the way you think."

"Does that mean you only love me for my brains?"

Damn. How was he supposed to answer that? He opted for the truth. "Hell, no. I'm pretty fond of all of your parts. And I believe your motor's already running, baby girl."

"Hmm. That's because you were right."

"About what?"

"I've been hot-wired."

He grinned. It was good to know he was right…at least occasionally.

Epilogue

NATALIE SWIPED a tear from her eye as Caitlyn and Cash rode off into the sunset in a white buggy pulled by a pair of white horses.

"Absolutely beautiful," Beverly said, looking at the carriage and dabbing at her eyes with a fine handkerchief. Scooter patted her on the shoulder and winked at Natalie.

"Y'all done good, Nat'lie and Cynthia."

"Thanks, Scooter," Natalie said, not quite believing that they'd actually pulled it off.

Was that a look that passed between Beau and Cynthia? They'd become as thick as thieves once Cynthia had decided Beau wasn't the bad guy.

"Why don't you and Beau take a walk down to the river and let me get on with the cleanup," Cynthia said. "You know I like this part."

"But—"

"Shoo. Go."

"Tell me what you want me to do," Tilson said. He and Cynthia had met when Cynthia came out to Belle Terre one day. The two had been inseparable since then.

"C'mon," Beau urged, wrapping an arm around Natalie's waist and leading her around the side of the house. Even after three months, his touch still thrilled her. She suspected it always would.

They strolled in silence past the white tent on the lawn where the orchestra was packing up, down the sloping green hill to the swing that hung from a cottonwood at the river's edge. Of one accord, they settled next to one another on the swing.

Beau dropped a kiss on the top of her head. "That was a helluva wedding you pulled off, baby girl."

She leaned her head into the crook of his shoulder and smoothed her fingers over the leg of his trousers. He was heart-stoppingly handsome in his black tux. There wasn't a woman at the wedding who hadn't given him the eye. And that was just what it was like to date a hot hunk of a man.

"It was, wasn't it? But *we* pulled it off. You did a fantastic job with Belle Terre. We make a pretty good team, you and I."

She'd wanted nothing more than to be the one walking down the aisle with him today. She'd never been more sure of anything in her life.

"The best." He absently stroked his finger along the ridge of her collarbone. She loved the fact that he was always touching her. "I'm guessing you're about to be swamped with business."

"I'm thinking so. If things go the way I think they

will, we'll need to start renovating the upstairs of the shop in a couple of months."

The sun was dipping low in the sky and a mosquito buzzed past her ear.

"I wanted to talk to you about that," he said. It was that tone she'd come to recognize—the one he used when he was about to try to manage her.

"Okay?"

"If we're teaming up, I figured this was appropriate."

He reached into the pocket inside his jacket, pulled out a rectangular, flat gift box and handed it to her. Not the ring box she would've liked to have seen, but he was definitely up to something.

Puzzled, she opened it and lifted the lid. She burst out laughing. A brand-spanking new paint scraper lay nestled in tissue paper, a red ribbon attached to the handle. "You're crazy."

"About you. It's engraved on the other side."

She flipped the scraper over. Inscribed on the blade was Natalie Stillwell. And there, attached to the red ribbon, a ring.

Her breath seemed to lodge in her throat, and for a few seconds she felt dizzy.

"Marry me." In typical, wonderful Beau Stillwell fashion, it was a directive rather than a question.

Her hands were so unsteady she couldn't untie the bow with the ring on it. "This is just a ploy to get me to move to Dahlia so you can sleep easy at night."

He grinned, taking the scraper from her and working

at the ribbon. "There you go, making everything hard again. And I told you from the beginning I was a selfish bastard. I want you where I can keep an eye on you." He sobered, freeing the ring from the ribbon. "I want you to be with me, looking at those hills every morning when we wake up and every night when we go to bed. I want us to have babies together and I want us to sit on that porch and grow old together."

"That's absolutely beautiful." She was about two seconds from tearing up.

"There's a theme there. Together. Say yes, Natalie."

"Yes, yes and yes." She held out her hand and he slipped the emerald-cut diamond onto her finger. A perfect fit.

* * * * *

In honor of our 60th anniversary,
Harlequin® American Romance® is celebrating by
featuring an all-American male each month,
all year long with
MEN MADE IN AMERICA!
This June, we'll be featuring American men
living in the West.

Here's a sneak preview of
THE CHIEF RANGER by Rebecca Winters.

Chief Ranger Vance Rossiter has to confront the
sister of a man who died while under Vance's
watch...and also confront his attraction to her.

"Chief Ranger Rossiter?" The sight of the woman who'd stepped inside Vance's office brought him to his feet. "I'm Rachel Darrow. Your secretary said I should come right in."

"Please," he said, walking around his desk to shake her hand. At a glance he estimated she was in her mid-twenties. Her feminine curves did wonders for the pale blue T-shirt and jeans she was wearing. "Ranger Jarvis informed me there's a young boy with you."

The unfriendly expression in her beautiful green eyes caught him off guard. "Yes," was her clipped reply. "When we arrived in Yosemite the ranger told me I couldn't go anywhere in the park until I talked to you first."

"That's right."

"Knowing you wanted this meeting to be private, he offered to show my nephew around Headquarters."

So this woman was the victim's sister… "What's his name?"

"Nicky."

The boy who haunted Vance's dreams now had a name. "How old is he?"

"He turned six three weeks ago. Were you the man in charge when my brother and sister-in-law were killed?"

"Yes. To tell you I'm sorry for what happened couldn't begin to convey my feelings."

The woman's gaze didn't flicker. "I won't even try to describe mine. Just tell me one thing. Was their accident preventable?"

"Yes," he answered without hesitation.

"In other words, the people working under you fell asleep on your watch and two lives were snuffed out as a result."

Hearing it put like that, he had to set the record straight. "My staff had nothing to do with it. I myself could have prevented the loss of life."

Ms. Darrow's expression hardened. "So you admit culpability."

"Yes. I take full blame."

A look of pain crossed over her features. "You can just stand there and admit it?" Her cry echoed that of his own tortured soul.

"Yes." He sucked in his breath.

"I work for a cruise line. Aboard ship, it's the captain's responsibility to maintain rigid safety regulations. If a disaster like that had happened while he was in charge he would have been relieved of his command and never given another ship again."

Rachel Darrow couldn't know she was preaching to the converted. "If you've come to the park with the intention of bringing a lawsuit against me for negligence, maybe you should." It would only be what he deserved.

"Maybe I will."

In the next instant, she wheeled around and hurried out of his office. Vance could have gone after her, but it would cause a scene, something he was loath to do for a variety of reasons. In the first place, he needed to cool down before he approached her again.

The discovery of the Darrows' frozen bodies had affected every ranger in the park. A little boy had been orphaned—a boy whose aunt was all he had left.

* * * * *

*Will Rachel allow Vance to explain—and
will she let him into her heart?
Find out in
THE CHIEF RANGER
Available June 2009 from
Harlequin® American Romance®.*

Copyright © 2009 by Rebecca Burton

We'll be spotlighting a different series every month
throughout 2009 to celebrate our 60th anniversary.

Look for Harlequin®
American Romance® in June!

Join us for a year-long celebration of the rugged
American male! From cops to cowboys—
Men Made in America has the hero
you've been dreaming about!

Look for

The Chief Ranger

by Rebecca Winters, on sale in June!

Bachelor CEO by Michele Dunaway	July
The Rodeo Rider by Roxann Delaney	August
Doctor Daddy by Jacqueline Diamond	September

www.eHarlequin.com HARBPA09

nocturne™

New York Times Bestselling Author

REBECCA BRANDEWYNE

FROM THE MISTS OF WOLF CREEK

Hallie Muldoon suspects that her grandmother
has special abilities, but her sudden death
forces Hallie to return to Wolf Creek, where
details emerge of a spell cast. Local farmer
Trace Coltrane and the wolf that prowls around
the farmhouse both appear out of nowhere, and
a killer has Hallie in his sights. With no other
choice, Hallie relies on Trace for help,
not knowing if the mysterious Trace is a
mesmerizing friend or a deadly foe....

Available June wherever books are sold.

www.paranormalromanceblog.com　　　　　SN61812

REQUEST YOUR FREE BOOKS!

2 FREE NOVELS PLUS 2 FREE GIFTS!

HARLEQUIN®

Blaze™

Red-hot reads!

YES! Please send me 2 FREE Harlequin® Blaze™ novels and my 2 FREE gifts (gifts are worth about $10). After receiving them, if I don't wish to receive any more books, I can return the shipping statement marked "cancel". If I don't cancel, I will receive 6 brand-new novels every month and be billed just $4.24 per book in the U.S. or $4.71 per book in Canada. Shipping and handling is just 25¢ per book. That's a savings of 15% or more off the cover price! I understand that accepting the 2 free books and gifts places me under no obligation to buy anything. I can always return a shipment and cancel at any time. Even if I never buy another book, the two free books and gifts are mine to keep forever.

151 HDN ERVA 351 HDN ERUX

Name	(PLEASE PRINT)	
Address		Apt. #
City	State/Prov.	Zip/Postal Code

Signature (if under 18, a parent or guardian must sign)

Mail to the **Harlequin Reader Service:**
IN U.S.A.: P.O. Box 1867, Buffalo, NY 14240-1867
IN CANADA: P.O. Box 609, Fort Erie, Ontario L2A 5X3

Not valid to current subscribers of Harlequin Blaze books.

Want to try two free books from another line?
Call 1-800-873-8635 or visit www.morefreebooks.com.

* Terms and prices subject to change without notice. Prices do not include applicable taxes. N.Y. residents add applicable sales tax. Canadian residents will be charged applicable provincial taxes and GST. Offer not valid in Quebec. This offer is limited to one order per household. All orders subject to approval. Credit or debit balances in a customer's account(s) may be offset by any other outstanding balance owed by or to the customer. Please allow 4 to 6 weeks for delivery. Offer available while quantities last.

Your Privacy: Harlequin Books is committed to protecting your privacy. Our Privacy Policy is available online at www.eHarlequin.com or upon request from the Reader Service. From time to time we make our lists of customers available to reputable third parties who may have a product or service of interest to you. If you would prefer we not share your name and address, please check here. ☐

HB09R

You're invited to join our Tell Harlequin Reader Panel!

By joining our new reader panel you will:

- Receive Harlequin® books—they are FREE and yours to keep with no obligation to purchase anything!
- Participate in fun online surveys
- Exchange opinions and ideas with women just like you
- Have a say in our new book ideas and help us publish the best in women's fiction

In addition, you will have a chance to win great prizes and receive special gifts! See Web site for details. Some conditions apply. Space is limited.

To join, visit us at
www.TellHarlequin.com.

THBPA0108

HARLEQUIN *Blaze*

COMING NEXT MONTH
Available May 26, 2009

#471 BRANDED Tori Carrington
Jo Atchison isn't your average cowgirl. She's rough, she's tough and she's sexy as hell. And regardless of the rules, she wants rancher Trace Armstrong. Luckily, Trace wants Jo, too. The only one not happy about it is Jo's volatile boyfriend….

#472 WHEN THE SUN GOES DOWN... Crystal Green
A trip to Japan on family business is just the chance Juliana Thompsen and Tristan Cole have been waiting for. They've been hopelessly in love with each other for years, but a family feud made a relationship impossible. Now they're alone, and they're going to experience *everything* they've missed. But will it be enough to last them a lifetime?

#473 UNDRESSED Heather MacAllister
Encounters
Take some naughty talk, add one *very* thin wall between the last dressing room in a bridal shop and a tuxedo boutique, and what do you have? The recipe for a happy marriage…and four very satisfied—and enlightened—couples. When you get this kind of tailoring, who needs a honeymoon?

#474 TWIN TEMPTATION Cara Summers
The Wrong Bed: Again and Again
Maddie Farrell has just learned she has a twin sister. And she's an heiress. *And* she's just had sex with the hot stranger in her bed! It must be a mistake. Right? Hmm—she might have to have more sex just to make sure….

#475 LETTERS FROM HOME Rhonda Nelson
Uniformly Hot!
Ranger Levi McPherson is getting some anonymous, red-hot love letters during his tour of duty! When he comes home on leave, he's determined to track down the mysterious author…and show her that actions speak louder than words.

#476 THE MIGHTY QUINNS: BRODY Kate Hoffmann
Quinns Down Under
Runaway bride Payton Harwell thinks she's hit rock bottom when she ends up in jail—in Australia! But then sexy rebel Brody Quinn bails her out and lets her into his home, his bed, his life. Only, Payton's past isn't as far away as she thinks it is….